A *PASSION* FOR
PASSION

A *PASSION* FOR PASSION

A DELIRIOUS LOVE LETTER TO ROMANCE

Alice Fraser

unbound

First published in 2025
Unbound
c/o TC Group, 6th Floor King's House, 9–10 Haymarket, London SW1Y 4BP

www.unbound.com

All rights reserved

Copyright © Alice Fraser, 2025

Illustrations © Alice Fraser, 2025

Internal covers on pages 18, 63, 102, 122, 167, 192 designed by Mecob, 2025.
Image credits: Jenny Le Blanc/Illustrated Romance, The Killion Group,
© Shutterstock.com and © iStockphoto

The right of Alice Fraser to be identified as the author of this work has been asserted in accordance with Section 77 of the Copyright, Designs and Patents Act, 1988. No part of this publication may be copied, reproduced, stored in a retrieval system, or transmitted, in any form or by any means without the prior permission of the publisher, nor be otherwise circulated in any form of binding or cover other than that in which it is published and without a similar condition being imposed on the subsequent purchaser.

A CIP record for this book is available from the British Library

ISBN 978-1-80018-362-9 (hardback)
ISBN 978-1-80018-363-6 (ebook)

Printed in Great Britain by Clays Ltd, Elcograf S.p.A

1 3 5 7 9 8 6 4 2

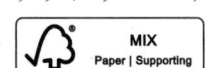

For Cordelia and Ivo

Contents

Foreword by Andy Zaltzman xiii
What Is This Book? 1
Are YOU a Romance Heroine? 7
Are YOU a Romance Hero? 12
Favourite Novels 13
Victorian / Industrial Revolution 15
    The Dim Menagerie 15
    The Heights of Longing 17
    The Duke's Tonic 20
    Dark Bridges of the Heart 22
But Why the Victorian Era? 24
The Regency 26
    The Earl-ish Duke's Half-Hungarian Headmistress 26
    The Wicked Wastrel 29
    Excavating Her Passion 32
    Down for the Count 35
But Why the Regency? 38
A Taxonomy of Dukes (incomplete) 41

Hero Jobs	46
Fantasy	48
The Dragon Lord's Lady	48
The Crystal Throne	52
The Crystal Staff	55
But Why Vampires?	57
But Why Half-Vampires?	59
Dark and Middle Ages	61
A Darkling Sail	61
The Piercing Falcon	64
Creatures: Werewolves	71
The Master-Laird's Wolf-Lord	71
Little Red Riding Werewolf	75
A Weekend with the Wolf	77
But Why Werewolves?	79
Leopard Shifters	81
Night Passions	81
Light Fingers in Darkness	84
But Why Sexiness?	86
Whither Hotness?	89
But Why Underwater Creatures?	91
Underwater	93
The Mantle of the Deep	93
A Veteran's Honour	95
King of the Gloom	97
The Wet Ones	99
Upside-Down Sex	101
America [Modern]	105
A Knight of Passion	105
Get Your Bits In	110

- Balls in the Air 112
- Fertilised in the Billionaire's Garden 113
- The Sorceror Next Door of My Dreams 114

What Is America? 117

America [Historical] 119
- The Femme Falcon 119
- A Cowboy Called Home 121

Novelty 124
- The Lost Duke 125
- We Made It One Night 129
- The Mob Boss's Captured Concubine 131
- A Hill to Call My Own 133

Create Your Own D'Ancey 135

Short Stories 138
- Once a Pond-er Time 138
- The Greek Baron's Pregnant Concubine and Other Short Stories 141

The Place of the Penis in Romance Novels 142
- Quiz Your Family 144

Sci-Fi / Future 145
- They Came From Above 145
- Star Crown 147
- Son of the King of the Gloom 149
- The Forgetful Prince's Heroic Seamstress 151

Time Travel 152
- The Quartzen Queendom 152
- Out of Time and in His Arms 154
- The Mannerly Match 158
- The Lost Post 160

LGBTQ+ 162
- The Lord and His Man 164

    Lord Pranceling's Redemption..166

    Storm in a TeaCount..169

    The Other Word for Ottoman... 171

Polyamory / Ménage à Trois... 173

    The Argument for Triangles... 173

    The SEALs' Sexy Seal..175

    Three's a Crowd..179

Unspecified Historical..181

    Luring the Laird...181

    Athenian Pirate Sexy Vampire Scoundrel Adventure................................ 183

    Legs in the Gloaming... 185

Christmas...188

    The Highland Laird's Christmas Miracle.....................................190

    The Call of the Christmas Supernova.. 193

Quizzes 195

    Quiz 1..196

    Quiz 2..199

Afterword 202

Fashion Tips..205

Encountering Romance 211

But Is D'Ancey LaGuarde Real?... 213

Academic Thoughts on Mystery 215

Postscript...218

Supporters 221

A Note on the Author 239

A *PASSION* FOR
PASSION

Foreword

When I heard that Alice Fraser had been selected to curate the long-awaited D'Ancey LaGuarde anthology, it all made perfect sense. Indeed, in retrospect, it was clear that this perfect meeting of creative minds would have happened years, perhaps even decades ago, if, for example, they had both been alive in the 1960s.

I first met Alice in 2017, when fate – in the form of me, looking for new co-hosts for *The Bugle* podcast – threw us together. Her linguistic ingenuity, satirical insight, vibrant ideas and fiercely intelligent brand of stupidity concocted a comedic cocktail that marked her out as different from at least 7 billion of the world's population, probably more. She rapidly became a staple of *The Bugle* co-host rotation, quite literally so, due to her ability to metaphorically hold things together.

What I had not expected was for Alice to introduce me to the oeuvre of Romance novel major leaguester D'Ancey LaGuarde. I had steered the ship of my life well clear of

Foreword

Romance novels, ever since a scarring incident at my all-boys school, in which I was forced to read five chapters of Dreville Featherwell's preternaturally graphic 1970s bodice-ripper *Midnight Gondola to Colombo* in front of a classroom of my teenaged peers and our strictly disciplinarian English teacher, Mrs Hawksbury-Jelks.

However, as arguably the world's leading LaGuardist scholar, Alice educated me to understand that the genre, when perpetrated by a Romancesmith of LaGuarde's dexterity and persistence, involved the stripping-off, not only of garments, but also of the layers of the human soul. This tome, surely destined to be regarded as the definitive LaGuarde collection, will take its rightful place in the Romance pantheon, to be read, enjoyed and cuddled as long as this famous species of ours retains an interest in the workings of its own fervid hearts.

Andy Zaltzman, July 2024

What Is This Book?

This book is a comedy about Romance. It's not a Romantic Comedy, though I'm hoping by the end you'll fall in love — with me — with Romance. This book is a tribute to the many works of D'Ancey LaGuarde. The vast majority of it will be synopses from the back covers of D'Ancey LaGuarde books, extracts from those books and contemplative essays on the genre.

D'Ancey LaGuarde is the alleged author of a series of books that have been appearing in my comedy for some years. Like Hamlet's father, it's a matter of opinion as to whether they exist or not, but real or not, *those* books are the sperm and egg from which *this* book springs, a triumphant baby, fully formed.*

---

*   I advertised these books on my podcasts *The Gargle* and *The Last Post*. *The Last Post* was a daily satirical news podcast I did in 2020 that was set in an alternate dimension. As the first 'spin-off' show from satirical juggernaut *The Bugle*, *The Last Post* was an extremely silly and joyous exercise in interdimensional newscasting, satire and comedy, and had a modest but

A Passion for Passion

Once every week or so on my podcasts, listeners would hear the fateful words, '. . . and a new novel is out by self-published Romance maven and online bestseller D'Ancey LaGuarde,' and I would read a summary of the plot of a book from an alternate universe in which the author LaGuarde is THE hugely famous, successful and influential writer.*

If we were to suggest, purely hypothetically, that all of the ads for all of these books and the very books themselves were fiction, a figment of my Science-Fiction-Fantasy-and-Romance-damaged imagination, then I would be obliged at this point to tell you the origin story of this book and its profoundly deranged commitment to the joyful silliness of Romance novel back-cover copy.

Of course, D'Ancey LaGuarde must be real, otherwise writing this whole book would be a completely off-the-rails exercise in taking a joke too far. But hypothetically, if the whole thing were a joke that *had* got significantly out of hand, I might roughly (but tenderly) place the origin of D'Ancey LaGuarde in a family holiday when I was about ten. We stayed in a place that had a bookshelf full of Romance novels: Mills & Boon, Harlequin – swooning women in the arms of various Fabios. (Fabiii? Fabiuses? Fabios, like octopuses, occupy an

---

extremely loving and loyal fanbase. Writing and performing it got me through the worst of the year that was 2020 (both emotionally and in terms of paying the rent).

* It is always convenient to situate your muses and heroes in an alternate dimension on the premise that if meeting your heroes ruins the halo, the opposite might also be true.

What Is This Book?

ambiguous linguistic position regarding plurality. Though the group noun for a lot of Fabios is a Clinch.) There were also shelves of Sci-Fi novels with anti-gravitationally well-endowed women in diaphanous togas standing on or before metal thrones, or dominating the foreground of alien landscapes and retro-futuristic spacecraft, and Fantasy novels showcasing extremely implausible dragons with abs. My twin brother and I would pick them off the shelves and solemnly read out the back covers to each other, one after the other, trying to keep a straight face, driving each other into wild fits of rib-wringing laughter. D'Ancey LaGuarde would be the distilled essence of those wild evenings of stupid joy. The ur-author or every guilty genre pleasure left on a holiday bookshelf. The unheimlich Frankensteining* of a thousand summer reads.

One result of that holiday activity was to give me a lifelong love of solemn silliness. A love of things where the goal is not that they achieve some high literary legitimacy, but just that they be the joyful thing they are, as hard as they can. It might have given me a strong feeling that joy and silliness *are enough* to make a thing worth it. I've never liked the phrase 'worth

---

* Actually, while some people use every reference to Frankenstein to wedge in the factoid that *actually* the monster is nameless and the *doctor* is called Frankenstein, and others might contend that *actually* the doctor is the real monster, I'd contend that the real monster is you for using the heartbreaking story of Frankenstein as a forum for pedantic point-scoring. If Victor Frankenstein is (as the monster contends) the father of the monster, then the monster's last name is also Frankenstein (and he doesn't have a first name). So there.

it'. What is 'it'? The 'it' you can make in New York? Is 'it' a pastrami bagel? Genre books, particularly Romance and the 'girly' sub genres of 'soft' Sci-Fi and Fantasy, ones that have characters and relationships, rather than just missions, revel in their tropes, play *with* their readers, and create a world in which we all consent for a while to the idea – however ridiculous – that everything can turn out alright in the end.

In being a tribute to D'Ancey LaGuarde, this book is a love letter to genre fiction in general, and Romance specifically. Romance is particularly maligned, even among genres, in part because it has traditionally and primarily been written by women and for women. The tropes and archetypes of even the silliest Romance are not inherently more masturbatory, predictable, self-indulgent or wish-fulfilment-y than, say, James Bond, but they are treated as dirty, dorky little secrets kept by naïve, silly, frumpy escapists. The magic trick of a Romance novel is that we know how it ends. We know who is going to end up together, usually from the first chapter. And yet, the author has to make it gripping. While we *know* they'll live happily ever after, we must *feel* at some point that the author can't possibly pull off the trick. That's art, telling people the punchline and still have it be surprising and delightful. All genre novels are essentially a little puzzle constructed of character and context. In Romance, seeing how the heroine solves her society's rules, her own character and the problem that is the hero, to get her to happily ever after is what draws the reader in. Worse even than their silliness, Romance novels have the distinction of being, about female joy, rather than female suffering.

What Is This Book?

Unlike most 'serious' art, which tends to revel in the femme misérable.

Perhaps that's a side reason for a lot of the mistrust of Romance. If a woman believes (even in some small, silly corner of her heart, even in the way that many men secretly half-believe they'd be quite good at being James Bond should the opportunity arise) that life could hold a gentle jacked cowboy with a huge and adoring penis who'd give up his glamorous life as an itinerant rodeo rider to help her start the animal sanctuary of her dreams, what does that mean for society? Or the dude she's with right now, who is insisting that it's just he doesn't know *how* to make dinner for the kids.

Even though the number of Romance novels sold is mind-bogglingly large, indulgence in Romance is seen as a slightly pathetic pursuit for silly single girls or, worse, ageing housewives. Mainly because anything that is enjoyed by ageing housewives or teenage girls is inherently silly-coded. Their taste cannot be good because, well . . . it's *their* taste.

We haven't come so far from the idea that women reading novels would make their wombs fall out or something equally hysterical. I don't want to pretend my job is changing the world, but I like to think that it is a little bit of pushback against the idea that women's pleasure is dangerous, that women's joy is naughty, that women's laughter is an act of rebellion.

Bringing D'Ancey to this universe has made me laugh from the beginning, in the way I used to laugh with my twin on holidays. Reading out the synopses on my podcasts felt like tapping into a place of childhood joy, as well as adult naughty silliness. I never expected those ads to 'hit' with the audience.

A Passion for Passion

They were for me. But then all of a sudden, lots of people said D'Ancey was for them, too. Enough that when this silly book was proposed, the pre-sales funded the production cost of the book inside four days.*

If you need a 'real' reason to read this book, let it be as a serious argument for the legitimacy of silly joy. But I'm here to tell you, you don't need a real reason.

Please feel free to read this book with legs open to the ridiculousness of Romance, quivering with yearning, wallowing in an unrestrained passion for passion, holding a boombox in the rain at midnight in the garden of your heart.

This book will give you a small taste of the vast D'Ancey LaGuarde oeuvre; enough, we hope, to let you understand why the works of D'Ancey LaGuarde have achieved enough momentum and force to break through the barriers between dimensions and penetrate our own. Our hope for this book is that you too receive full-body thrills the next time you see a shelf full of 'silly' books or hear the fateful words, '. . . and a new novel is out by self-published Romance maven and online bestseller D'Ancey LaGuarde.'

---

*   Thank you.

Are YOU a Romance Heroine?

Before we collectively bite our lower lip and plunge tenderly into the quivering body of this work, I urge you to situate yourself within the genre by discovering if you are a Romance heroine or not.

Romance heroines! What even is one and are you she?*

If you are wondering if you know someone who is a Romance heroine,† or are suddenly suspecting, while being

---

* For the purposes of the following passages, a Romance heroine need not be a woman, but as the origin of the type was in a rich soil bed of heteronormativity, we'll stick with the feminine pronoun.

† The easiest way to find a Romance heroine, of course, is to be a Romance hero, and look at who you're suddenly pressing passionately against a tree or horse as their creamy bosom strains at their surprisingly rippable bodice. If she haunts your dreams and makes you revise extremely fundamental elements of your day-to-day character and behaviour, like turning you from a rake to a family man, or a heartless banker to a hopeless romantic, you've probably found one. (Which one? THE one.) If you

A Passion for Passion

kissed in a hedge, fingered against a wall or pressed up against a massive erection on a horse, that YOU might be a Romance heroine, here are some good rules of thumb.

Part of this process of elimination will be determined by whether you live in the past, the present, the future or a fantasy realm. Differing levels of sassiness, competence and violence are likely to apply.

- If you are living in the Regency period, you can basically assume you're a Romance heroine.* The period seems to have been entirely peopled by incredibly attractive people fraughtly falling in love with one another over fluttering fans in manors, ballrooms or Bath.
- If you are, however, living in the Victorian period, you are *probably* a Romance heroine, but you may also be a ragged lady, trying to feed a bottle of gin to a baby, whose lot in life is to mistrustfully open a door to give someone directions. Check your person for bottles of gin to triangulate.

---

would like to find out whether you're a Romance hero, please turn to the next chapter, but probably hold your place in this one with a finger.

* You *could* be a shrew or a scheming dowager, a vapid and vain heiress or possibly a wrung-out, fretful and sexless governess of an irritating nervous bent. But let's assume for the sake of goodwill that you're full of spunk or desperately put upon and therefore almost definitely about to be swept out of your comfortable life by the love of your dreams.

Are YOU a Romance Heroine?

- If you find yourself looking in the mirror, cataloguing your features as though someone might be listening to your inner monologue and imagining exactly what kind of hot you are.[*] But, no matter how beautiful you are in the mirror, you must never be aware of your own beauty. If you know you are beautiful, looking in a mirror, then you are probably a villain, or a beautiful but selfish little sister due for a reckoning, probably by seeing your plain but sensible sister run off with and win the heart of a marquis.[†] Sorry.[‡]
- You can be made to feel beautiful in the eyes of the hero. Other men finding you beautiful makes you feel uncomfortable. Sorry.
- If you're not stunningly beautiful (when taken out of comparison with your outrageously beautiful but shallow or lovely yet stupid sister), you could have horrible disfiguring scars that are actually quite superficial and do nothing to disguise your beauty

---

[*] Same old flaming hair and boring violet eyes. You remember how your brothers used to tease you for the sprinkling of golden freckles across your pert nose.

[†] This is the kind of book where the sensible elder sister tries to lure the marquis away from her silly but beautiful younger sister, and then they have to get married because his idiosyncratic morals require that while he can slut around, he cannot ruin an innocent, so they get married and THEN they fall in love.

[‡] You are allowed to think you are beautiful if someone's put you in a ball-gown for the first time. But you have to be surprised about it.

A Passion for Passion

to the many men and women who are immediately in love with you and/or want to kill you.
- You are *almost certainly* in your mid-twenties.
- If you're not in your mid-twenties, whatever age you are, be assured you don't look it.
- Nobody who has any moral goodness can hate you. Nobody good can hate a heroine. They might mistrust or be threatened by you, but by the end of the story they will begrudgingly respect you or become your best friend, receiving as a reward a book of their own later in the series.
- You have an infallible lodestone located alternately in your heart or your crotch that will tell you who to fall in love with, even if you initally encounter him while fully believing him to be the monster who ate your parents and is trying to annihilate your village, small business or virginity.
- Instantly wanting to bang someone is a valid cue that they are actually not evil, because they can't be evil because they're the love of your life, and therefore you can assume that although all the information you have ever been given — and evidence and experience — would indicate they are evil, your irresistible urges mean they must either be misunderstood or can be won to the side of righteousness by the sexy love of a good woman.
- Any sex you have with the hero must be light-bendingly good, the best sex you've ever had, on a sliding scale increasing in sexiness towards

Are YOU a Romance Heroine?

Happily Ever After, at which point the author ceases to attempt to even describe how good the sex is, presumably because they've run out of horny words and it becomes impossible to continue describing the increasing excellence of a penis on an exponential curve.*

- You have eyes and hair of some specialness, not unlike what a dreamy but socially awkward teen dreaming of a life writing romantic fantasies in Romance and Fantasy might imagine.†
- Even if you're captured in a horrible dungeon with no water for washing, you'll come out looking quite good and bang-able, and will be on board with a full-on make-out session surprisingly quickly, regardless of trauma.

---

* Though of course some penises are in themselves an exponential curve.

† I was this teen. I used to skip class to sit in the library and read various unwholesome texts. Eventually they gave me a badge and the courtesy title 'roving library monitor' which meant I'd occasionally reshelve some maths books in between reading sexy dragon novels.

Are YOU a Romance Hero?

No. Sorry.

No really, I'm sorry.

No matter how many abs you have, you don't have as many and they aren't as rippling as those of a true Romance hero. A true Romance hero is an impossible paradox. He must be incomprehensibly oblivious to the needs of his fated match, his own emotions and the capacity of open communication to solve a myriad of relationship problems, and then suddenly obsessively and instinctively capable of fulfilling his heroine's emotional and physical needs once the requirements of narrative tension are climactically released. Are *you* a conceptual paradox capable of turning yourself emotionally inside-out like a sock finding its pair? While maintaining 6 per cent body fat? NO? I thought not.

Favourite Novels

Only a small sampling of D'Ancey LaGuarde texts has ever made its way into our dimension, and those books have often been incomplete.* The vast majority of D'Ancey's books that we've found come through Henrietta Schliemann's† famous excavation of back-cover blurbs – a stratum of interdimensional books uncovered at an ancient Barbara Cartland burial site. Unfortunately for this dimension, however, during

---

* It is impossible, in this dimension, to be a D'Ancey LaGuarde completist. Aside from the fact that only a small scattering of the writings has made it across to our universe, D'Ancey writes faster than most people can read. It is alleged that inside D'Ancey's abode, each room contains a secretary, and that LaGuarde roams whimsically between the rooms, dictating at least five books at once. Some academics and experts claim they can tell the 'flavour' of the room each book was written in, and that, for example, all the modern supernaturals were transcribed by the secretary in the guest powder room. This cannot be verified and is generally considered to be boasting.

† No relation to famous grave-scrabbler Heinrich Schliemann.

the process of these books' journey between the unknown stanzas of the multiverse, something had rendered the pages themselves completely coagulated and incomprehensible. The books, displayed in the British Museum of Sexy Texts (right next to the naughtiest *Venus de Whipped Cream and Milo*), are completely unopenable.

They are beautifully decorated bricks, through the covers of which the best radiographic imaging can make no headway. But here are some of the best of the back blurbs of these beloved texts which broke through the cultural zeitgeist.* I have included clarifying commentary and context by D'Ancey where relevant, and by me where tempted.

---

* Causing comment, question or mass orgy, according to the police.

Victorian / Industrial Revolution

THE DIM MENAGERIE
[Medical, Victorian]

The Dim Menagerie is a violent, sexy and occasionally violently sexy instalment in LaGuarde's bestselling 'Hustle and Bustle' series of Georgian/early Victorian period Romance Thrillers with a supernatural twist.

Set in the mean streets of a rapidly industrialising London, *The Dim Menagerie* sweeps you into a world of coal and corsets.

Devin is the bastard son of a duke, forging his own way in the emerging world of science. Half-vampire, half-Victorian doctor, he's got his hands full figuring out the implications of germ theory while lusting for the blood of his patients. But there is something missing. Until, that is, he meets a lady being set upon by footpads in a dark alleyway and rescues her with his sword stick.

A Passion for Passion

Violet is a sassy suffragette with an anachronistic vocabulary and an elasticated corset . . . and amnesia. She doesn't need a man, but she can't remember why.

As Devin nurses her back to health, they fight the passion rising between them. But they can't fight the passion rising between them! And when Violet continues to be the subject of assassination attempts, they must track down the source of her mysterious diplomatic enemy and solve a plot to bring down the government . . . while also having sex.

Will Devin overcome his vampiric bloodlust and meet with his estranged father (now on his deathbed)? Will Violet overcome her violent fear of handwashing[*] and marry a doctor?

With a charming cameo by Violet's godfather, celebrity bridge-builder Isambard Kingdom Brunel, and a forty-page lecture on Joseph Lister's 'Principles of Sanitation', the *Guardian* called *The Dim Menagerie* 'a period piece that leaves a stain' and *The Times* called it 'the most graphic description of a Victorian-era penis surgery we've ever read'.

Available now in all bus terminals and airport bathrooms.

---

[*] Induced by an excessively vigilant governess who told her that washing your hands would attract the man of your dreams, which to a six-year-old Violet who dreamed mainly about the terrifying old man behind the counter at the bread shop seemed like an extremely negative outcome.

Victorian / Industrial Revolution

THE HEIGHTS OF LONGING
[Hot Air Balloons, Victorian]

The Heights of Longing *is a standalone in LaGuarde's 'Those Magnificent Men' series of standalone novels about Victorian aerialists, with an Industrial Revolution twist.*

Jack Haggerty is the king of the sky; a well-known exhibition aerialist and hot air balloon exhibitionist, he's got room in his heart only for his altitudinous ambitions and the clouds. His balloon is his mistress and the winds are his other mistresses.

Sangeetha is the illegitimate daughter of a wealthy East India Company partner, sent to London to earn her stripes running the books of her father's silk warehouse.

Jack's got a head for heights and thighs to swoon for. Sangeetha's got a head for business and a bottom for adventure. When Jack comes in to finger her silks, it's lust at first sight.

But the course of true love never did have a hitch-free launch. Jack is pursued by a newspaper journalist seeking a sensational headline, sky-high saboteurs, and thrill-seeking women dazzled by his celebrity (and his thighs). Meanwhile Sangeetha's hand in marriage is ruthlessly bartered for by a rival cloth house's boorish yet lordly owner's vile viscount son, whose offer represents both her father's approval and a way to enter the highest echelons of British society.

When a lustful aerialism fangirl's tangled scheme goes awry, Sangeetha finds herself literally caught up in a runaway

The HEIGHTS of Longing

She's getting carried away... by a balloon... and also by passion!

D'Ancey LaGuarde

Victorian / Industrial Revolution

hot air balloon incident with a hysterical teen, an outraged viscount and the one man she knows she shouldn't let ruffle her bustle. Reputation compromised mid-air, crash-landing in a village, abandoned by her horrible fiancé who elopes with the teen, with Jack injured in the groin and feverish from chivalrously giving her his coat, she must nurse this wounded yet muscular aerialist back to health in a rustic inn. Readers will adore the scenes in which she soothes his fevered groin and figures out how to save her father's business prospects.

The Heights of Longing is available at altitude and up the back of all respectable bustles.[*]

---

[*] Constantly plagued by the whims and scrums of publishing houses, D'Ancey's insistence on self-publication has been one of the ingredients that has left most LaGuarde scholars baffled as to how to complete a bibliography of all the work. Some books are available only by the light of the full moon, others only in truck-stop bathrooms or under trees that look like they've got faces in them. Very few are available from reputable bookshops, and often those are reprints rather than originals.

A Passion for Passion

THE DUKE'S TONIC
[Factory Owner, Victorian, Malarial]

The Duke's Tonic *is the next in LaGuarde's critically bemused Victorian Romance Thriller series with a supernatural twist.*

Reginalda is an American heiress visiting London to check on her family's investments. She sticks out like a sore thumb because she's too sassy for England's refined upper class, and she scandalises the whole haut ton with her sassy American-ness and her creamy breasts. The last thing she wants is a man who would check her reckless ways but when she's taken hostage by the sinister Hellfire Club during a scandalous game of cards, she swears she'll marry the first man to rescue her.

Lachlan is the bastard son of a duke, recently back from the subcontinental colonies and disillusioned with the life of the British aristocracy.

He spends his days secretly doing shamefully un-aristocratic business activities – navigating industrial property investments in London's commercial underbelly, disguised as a merely fabulously wealthy merchant – and his nights playing cards with the notorious Hellfire Club, while spying on the sleazeballs and villains of the nobility for the Crown.

Balancing his responsibilities as an espionage agent with his job as an industrial innovator and investor, Lachlan's secret life hides a dark secret. During his time in the colonies he was bitten by an infected mosquito and now he's half-man, half-malaria victim. He's sworn to avoid a loveless

Victorian / Industrial Revolution

marriage like the one his father had, and he fears his diagnosis will chase away willing women, but loneliness circles his soul like a mosquito at night until he stumbles upon a captive Reginalda.

Enraged by her creamy breasts, Lachlan has had it up to his impeccably tied cravat with the infuriating heiress and ragefully saves her from his criminal frenemies.

Clad only in scandalous nightgowns they have a disastrous smooching argument that leads to them falling through a rickety ceiling into Lady Herefordshire's Annual Rout. Driven into a hasty marriage by her foolhardy vow and the damage to her reputation, Lachlan and Reginalda must negotiate their newly married state, access sufficient quantities of quinine to achieve a therapeutic effect, unmask the ancient Hellfire Club members and negotiate a leasehold contract... while also having sex.

The Times called *The Duke's Tonic* 'an extremely sexually aggressive depiction of Victorian property contract negotiations'.

The *Guardian* called it 'a last stop on the road to literary legitimacy for LaGuarde'.

A Passion for Passion

DARK BRIDGES OF THE HEART
[Railway, Victorian]

A *supernatural Romance Period Thriller,* Dark Bridges of the Heart *is third in the 'Tycoons and Bonnets Railway Shenanigans' series. A slow-burn guardian-to-lovers tale set in a world of repressed emotions, forbidden-yet-fated love and canny infrastructure investment.*

Delighlah is an orphaned aristocrat and student at the prestigious Pinkerton Academy for Female Girls but she's hiding a dark secret. When she's expelled for burning down the school in a freak arson accident, she's claimed by her mysterious guardian, Declan.

Declan is the man of her dreams . . . literally. He is the man who appears each night in her unconscious to build sensuous load-bearing structures in her mind.

At first, he just seemed like a very handsome and mysterious guardian with the kind of dark backstory that makes him interestingly broken but in a sexily fixable way, but he's so much more. His dark backstory also involves a dangerous secret from his past that's casting a shadow over his future! And what's his connection with the prophecy that was tattooed on Delighlah's left shoulder as a baby? And who does baby tattoos? And why do Delighlah and Declan have the same dream whenever they're forced (by circumstances) into sharing a bedroom (which happens surprisingly often even though they're both wary of attachment)?*

---

* Variously by a storm, an overbooked inn, and a 'lost in the forest and

Victorian / Industrial Revolution

Declan is done with love; he's been hurt too many times. As a half-cursed elf dream lord, half-Victorian railway bridge architect he's seen the worst humanity has to offer.

He's planning on just collecting his ward and being coldly detached in an irresistibly brooding manner but the moment he sees her, he's overwhelmed with attraction and memories of the prophecy that he found on a piece of paper under a bridge on the day her parents died, the same day he cast his elf lord heritage aside and swore to marry a mortal.

He wants her but he can't have her for reasons that don't hold up to much scrutiny.

He's too troubled by his dark past and the fact that her dad was his boss at the railway bridge architecture firm, which creates a sense of feudal loyalty that would be offended by his banging the boss's daughter, however much she might be pressing herself up against him at night, getting caught in rainstorms in her nightgown and sharing vulnerable secrets while holding his hand at a nighttime construction site.

A steamy tale with a heartwarming cameo from Delighlah's godfather Isambard Kingdom Brunel, who teaches the troubled pair that sometimes all you need to do to solve an age-old curse is build a bridge and have sex on it.

Dark Bridges of the Heart is available now in all good online supernatural Romance Period Thriller stores and moving baggage carousels.

---

fallen into a river' incident that requires them to huddle for warmth in a conveniently-abandoned-yet-moderately-well-equipped rustic forest cabin, and Delighlah having a nightmare that requires him to hold her comfortingly through the night.

But Why the Victorian Era?

A period of heaving change and heaving bosoms, the Victorian era is known for being both bustling and full of bustles.* It's also a great place in time to set a Romance.† With traditional class barriers breaking up in the face of new industrial innovations and money moving in and out of new hands, there are many cracks and footholds for exciting and eccentric heroes and heroines to flourish. A queen on the throne meant the place of women in society was being

---

*   A sort of pre-Kardashian way to push out the back of a skirt.

†   Historian Greg Jenner says, 'The Victorian era shouldn't be considered a single coherent era; we only call it that because the Victorians called themselves Victorians, but comparing 1837 to 1901 is like chalk and cheese,' which is all well and good, but for the purposes of Romance, the broad span of time gives an author plenty of cultural wiggle room. Also, you could easily interchange chalk and cheese in a discussion about what the moon might be made of.

But Why the Victorian Era?

harrumphingly debated,* and horizons open for the adventurous Historical Romance writer where both prudish social pressures and risk-taking train-carriage-riding-sex-having adventures are suddenly available.†

In an age that straddled technology and tradition, modesty and rebellion, suffrage and repression, staid traditionalists and chaotic innovators, carriages and gaslight and electricity and the telegraph and public transport and the X-ray, Victorian settings invite the explorer to imagine other kinds of straddling. Also, trousers for men were looser fitting, and who can say what that affords room to grow?‡

---

* The real history of the women's suffrage movement and the expansion of opportunities for education into the lower classes made a good crack through which a modern writer might wedge some not entirely repugnant values into the heroine's ideas about what she might aim for in life.

† Though all credit should go to Romance readers, whose ability to suspend their disbelief rivals the flotation capacity of the most dashing of hot air balloonists.

‡ A penis? A penis.

The Regency*

THE EARL-ISH DUKE'S
HALF-HUNGARIAN HEADMISTRESS
[Second-Chance Romance, Ghost Vase]

The Earl-ish Duke's Half-Hungarian Headmistress *is a passionate tale set in the Regency period of England.*

After one passionate waltz at a country ball he had been accidentally trapped at, following a multiple horse collision that caused traffic delays a decade ago, the virile vagabond aka Gloucesterton, Earl of Duke, never forgot Mallory, the intelligent, witty and forbidden daughter of his family's worst enemy (Klaus the exiled Hungarian viscount) whom he courted and then spurned when he discovered her parentage. However, since suffering a disastrous marriage to a wife who

---

* Regency in Romance can be more of a vibe than a period and includes Georgian Era / Long Regency generally.

The Regency

turned out to be a haunted vase, the Earl of Duke has vowed never to succumb to the temptation of love again. Anulling his disastrous first marriage, he's left his half-ghost daughter to the tender mercies of feckless relatives and has taken to the high seas to bury his heartbreak in smuggling until the day an unexpected captive turns out to be the one woman (other than his vase-wife) who still haunts his dreams.

Reputation ruined after being trapped into a compromising position by her Hungarian viscount father's second worst enemy, Mallory has spent the past seven years as a governess patiently working to re-establish her character and hoping to finance a school for disgraced girls.

Though she can't rid herself of the foolish dreams in which a mysterious dancing partner waltzes her away from all her problems and onto his muscled horse. He took her heart with him when he scornfully left the country ball.

Over the years Mallory has played the part of the perfect governess but after overhearing a treason plot threatening her Hungarian viscount father, she deliberately allows herself to be kidnapped. When she wakens on the ship of the man who broke her heart, the virile vagabond tempts Mallory with a smouldering but restrained passion, and all the ship's biscuits she can eat. Despite temptation and some full-body contact astern, Mallory resists the powerful lust of the Earl of Duke, and convinces him to forgive her wayward father, who had been led astray from the path of virtue by excessive card-playing.

Acknowledging the danger of the passion that rages between them whenever they are together, he returns her to shore, stirred but essentially unravished. She is left with a bag of gold and the offer of a carte blanche, he with bags full of unexpressed longing and unvenged vengeance.

With the pirate earl's ill-gotten gains, Mallory has finally acquired enough money to finance her respectable school for disgraced girls, but she is torn by the offer of sexy pirate passion. She wants him, but she knows she can't be an earl's mistress and a headmistress at the same time. When the Earl of Duke's half-ghost daughter arrives at the stroke of midnight in her half-built school asking to enrol, the two must find out whether their true love can overcome the terrible past, the sulky sabotage of a half-ghost, half-teenager, and her Hungarian father's Magyar disapproval?

The Regency

THE WICKED WASTREL
[Regency, Kleptomania, Marriage of Convenience]

The Wicked Wastrel *is the third in LaGuarde's 'Harrowed Heroes' series of Regency Romance Thrillers with a supernatural twist.*

Dominic is a scandalous peer of the realm. Wealthy, titled and dangerous, he can have any woman he wants and he's bored of dodging matchmaking mammas and desperate damsels trying to trick him into marriage. Until one night when his carriage breaks down on the side of the road and he is helped by a passing governess, travelling alone to a family estate in Kent.

Elizabeth is the impoverished and orphaned daughter of a duke, making ends meet in the genteel occupation of governess, though she finds it difficult to be hired by the governessless because she's too sexy for governessness.

Elizabeth knows how to protect her reputation and isn't usually the type to court danger, but when she sees the muscular baron waiting by the side of the road she impulsively rescues him drawn to his dapper aura and his muscled forearms.

What harm can there be in an afternoon of unchaperoned but civilised conversation with a handsome stranger? A last freedom before settling down to a life of drudgery, wiping children and blackboards. But then her carriage breaks down and they must spend the night unchaperoned, huddling for warmth in the carriage and nobly resisting the magnetism that quivers meaningfully in the box (of the vehicle). Rescued at dawn by a passing aristocratic hunting party, society and honour demand that they wed. Dominic proposes a sexless marriage because he hated his horrible father and fears perpetuating a cycle of aristocracy,* but how can he resist the luscious auburn locks and creamy breasts of an innocent new wife, especially when she keeps having nightmares that mean he has to manfully hold her until dawn while ignoring the potent erection that would reveal his longing to anyone more educated in the art of banging than the innocent Elizabeth?

She doesn't know what an erection is, but she'll soon find out.†

Elizabeth may be an orphaned governess unlearned in the amorous arts but she's got a library of wastrel-grade erotic etchings and the horn to learn. When she sees her handsome new husband she feels throbbings in places she never knew could throb! What is a lady to do with her hot horny husband when he has said he doesn't want to bed her despite his promiscuous past because he fears banging the one woman he loves and she does know about consent even if she doesn't know about erections. Can she reveal her family curse, the thing that's giving her nightmares, the curse in her blood of being descended on her rascally mother's side from a family of sleep-thieves and night-kleptomaniacs?‡ Or will Dominic only find out when she accidentally steals his heart?

---

* There are no medium-grade parents in Romance.

† By reading about it in a book! She *is* a governess after all.

‡ The Regency was big on inherited sin, and not so big on understanding the science of genetics.

The Regency

Together, they must reveal their deepest insecurities and solve a rash of robberies while also not having sex* in a number of very intensely sexy ways.

---

*   This depends on how you define sex.

A Passion for Passion

EXCAVATING HER PASSION
[Paeleontology, Academic Rivals-to-Lovers]

Excavating Her Passion *is the fourth in the 'Bluestockings on Bedknobs' series of sexy science stories, rated what looks like three red-hot throbbing chillies on the hotness-ometer. A woman-in-STEM, nemeses-to-lovers Historical Romance with a supernatural twist, set in the early paleontological era of Georgian history.*

Merrin is the daughter of an eccentric academic lord in the wilds of Cornwall. She roams the beaches collecting bones from the cliffs and dunes and ignoring the boners of the local gentlemen. Buried in her books and theories, she fully intends to remain a bluestocking spinster, publishing scientific papers under her father's name.

Fox is the disgraced Earl of Mertonshireham. Condemned by society decades ago for running off with a married woman, he set his sights on further shores and has become a renowned Egyptologist, rejected by proper society but followed with lascivious interest by the haut ton for his infamously sexy Egyptology.

When he returns to Cornwall for important but unspecified reasons, he arranges to meet the reclusive dinosaur excavator whose papers he has been reading and refuting in the Royal Society of Old Stuff journals.*

---

* Putting the peer into peer reviews since 1790.

The Regency

Welcomed by the butler and the lord he believes to be his scientific interlocutor, Fox excuses himself to prepare an anachronistically enlightened and sensitive exegesis on the ethics of excavating mummies, which he plans to deliver over dinner. As he roams the beaches in anticipation of this meeting of scientific minds, he stumbles across a windswept goddess with her skirts hiked up, and seized with passion he offers to carry her up the cliff in return for a gentlemanly smooch. Merrin, stunned by the magnetic attraction she feels for this nice-smelling ruffian, is certain she, as a bluestocking, will never know the touch of a man, accepts the smooch for reasons of purely scientific research.

They are carried away on a wave of lustful but tastefully scientific experimental mutual fingering until the cumulative influence of sand and the impact of a sudden wet seagull recalls them both to their duties.

Returning to what they suddenly both realise is the same house, they must each face the fact that the person they thought merely a sexy beach stranger is their scientific frenemy and intellectual equal.

Will Merrin be able to look past Fox's smirched past and her own plans for a lonely independent life to accept a future of love and Egyptology? Will Fox be able to accept the fiery masculine science brain behind her lushly feminine lady face and deep, expressive boobs?

You'd think it would be a fairly soluble problem, but there's also a smuggling ring, ghosts and the return of Fox's married alleged ex-lover whom he turns out to have actually been rescuing from an abusive husband because actually, he was always too noble and so on and so forth but now she wants his help again and maybe also to bang him.

Will Merrin and Fox be able to solve mysteries, histories, social expectations and their deeply unscientific need to bang each other in increasingly precarious and unlikely locations until love, like dinosaurs, finds a way?

Find out in *Excavating Her Passion*, available in all 3.5-star rated bookshops and under the crust of slightly rained-on sand dunes.

The Regency

DOWN FOR THE COUNT
[Fairy Tale, Vampire, Regency Gothic]

Down for the Count *is the fourteenth in D'Ancey LaGuarde's 'Regency Gothic Remote Castle Fairy Tale Longings' series of Regency fairy tale reboots set in remote gothic castles.*

Eccentric lord Gerdidian Countington III is the disgraced son of a vampire count.

He fears nothing but love and mistrusts women, because his mother fell in love and ran away with the butler instead of teaching him how to respect females.[*] **He also always insists on opening his own doors because he'll never trust a butler again.**

Half-vampire aristocrat, half-professor (the black robe does double duty), he suppresses his lust for blood with his hunger for teaching mathematics.[†] Sick of the debauched

---

[*] Men who are mostly perfect but afraid of love are a common ocurrence in Romance, because it is an easier problem to solve in a narrative than 'hideous stench' or 'is a bore, too influenced by manosphere podcasts and DIY home testosterone injections'.

[†] Some scholars have drawn attention to the similarity of Gerdidian with Prince-Count Bloodmaths in *The Wet Ones*. This is because D'Ancey is drawing on a familiar vampire myth, which is that vampires can be distracted from their prey by giving them something small to count, often rice or sand. The fairy tales often use the device in stories where the vampire is a villain, and will be defeated by obsessively counting the many small things until the sun rises. Other than an early representation of arithmomania or OCD, this trope has appeared in modern vampire fiction

entertainments of the Regency vampire court, he retreats to his father's country estate to wrestle alone with his dark passions.

Cassandra is the outcast daughter of a country gentleman, cursed by a witch to spend only nights in her true form of a tall, golden-haired maiden, and her days in the form of a giant bird.

Shot from the sky by a hunter, she crash-lands in Gerdidian's remote castle as the sun sets and the reclusive mathematician finds himself with an injured beauty on his hands. Her low self-esteem about her height as a lady and her daily bird curse draw out a protective side in Gerdidian and he longs to claim her as his eternal mate. As Cassandra recuperates under this mysterious mathematician's meticulous care, she is struck by the contrast between his cold demeanour, his warm hands and his hot penis.

But under the threat of being disinherited by his father, can Gerdidian offer her anything more than a brief though passionate affair to make her stay? Cassandra knows her bird curse can be broken only by love's true sex and she refuses the count's heir's penis unless he can promise to love her.

All she wants is somewhere to call home but she cannot accept a loveless marriage with a man who's constantly running to get the door, and Gerdidian's fears of love and butlers drive her from his side.

When the count, Gerdidian's father, dies unexpectedly in a

---

even in our universe, where the best representation is probably Count von Count, from *Sesame Street*.

The Regency

mass vampire slaying, Gerdidian becomes Count Countington and inherits a fortune. When he returns to the ballrooms of London and the lecture halls of the Royal Academy with his breakthrough mathematical formula, he finds Cassandra the tall toast of the town, and engaged to a wealthy popinjay. Count must win back Cassandra's affection and together break her curse with love's true sex.

But Why the Regency?

The British Regency spanned just slightly less than a decade,* but like the hands of a duke spanning the waist of a swooning damsel, it has had a disproportionately large and lingering impact on the romantic imagination.†

So much Romance has been set in the Regency period that it has generated its own alternate timeline of history, which forks from our own and contains an historically unlikely

---

* 1811 to 1820, though for the purposes of Romance, we can consider the genre as spanning the 'long Regency' from around 1795 to the coronation of Victoria. And of course, most modern Romances are not set in the time period of the Regency so much as they are set in the fairly inaccurate fictional land of The Regency generated by the concentrated horniness of generations of writers and readers imagining it really hard.

† The masculine hands spanning a mini-waist as a shorthand for how attractive a woman is in Romance has fallen out of favour in the last ten or fifteen years; modern heroines are somewhat more robustly middled, and presumably less likely to snap, but we assume that the man-hand sizes have remained of much the same sort of Jack Reacher proportions.

But Why the Regency?

number of unmarried dukes being pressured into marriage by their families, gently bred girls seeking a living as governesses to the adorable but challenging offspring of recently bereaved marquises, and wide-eyed wards to grumpy viscounts who didn't want the responsibility of guardianship, and will have to clean up their rakish ways in order to responsibly marry off the young women they suddenly realise they desire above all things but are too debauched by their life choices to ever win.

All good genre novels are essentially little puzzles constructed of character and world; in Romance, seeing how the heroine solves her society's rules, her own character and the problem that is the hero to get to her *happily ever after* at the centre of the maze is what draws a reader in.*

The Regency is a particularly good period for setting a fantastic trap for a heroine.

You've got arranged marriages, rules of conduct, a hyper-wealthy aristocracy, rigid class divides, sparkling wit, horses, guns, swords, land-based old money, trade and commercial new money, strict chaperones, enforced modesty, scandal, religion and sexy footmen.

The Regency aristocratic high society is, at least in Romance novels, a location in which someone in a lovely dress

---

* Jane Austen, actually writing in the period, and Georgette Heyer, revolutionising historical fiction – a previously very masculine field – by making a whole subgenre that centred female desires and experiences, are two of the most influential mothers of Romance, and both used the strict structures of the society at the time to create the traps and puzzles their heroines had to escape if they were to achieve a Happily Ever After.

might meet meaningful eyes across a ballroom and touch gloved hands with as much sexy intensity as might be had in a full introductory bang.

D'Ancey LaGuarde's take on Regency Romance is both more relentlessly graphic and more pointlessly accurate than any other writer. No other Regency Romance writer will so accurately describe era-specific toilet habits, nor so passionately explore exactly which popular carriage of the time would be most conducive to a mobile, fully nude make-out session on a rutted highway.* LaGuarde's Regency protagonists range from same-sex lovers to cross-class canoodlers, to time-travelling mistresses, and the true D'Ancey reader embraces them all.

---

* Yes.

A Taxonomy of Dukes (incomplete)

For the purposes of this list it is important to clarify that not all dukes are dukes, and also not all dukes are dukes. Which is to say not every heroic love interest in period dramas will technically be a duke or even have a title; though it's likely that if he doesn't have a title, he'll have a nickname, and if he doesn't have a nickname indicating some level of status, he probably secretly has the right to a title. If he is a fisherman, he will be the most fishermanly: the Duke, as it were, of Fishermen.

Conversely, not everyone with the title of duke in a Romance has the qualities of a duke, which is to say there are plenty of old unattractive dukes, with no abs at all, and they are of no interest to us, except insofar as they might be usefully boring in a scene, or a villain, or the fate intended for an innocent girl by her scheming or well-meaning or well-meaningly-scheming parents.

That said, you know a duke when you see one, or at the

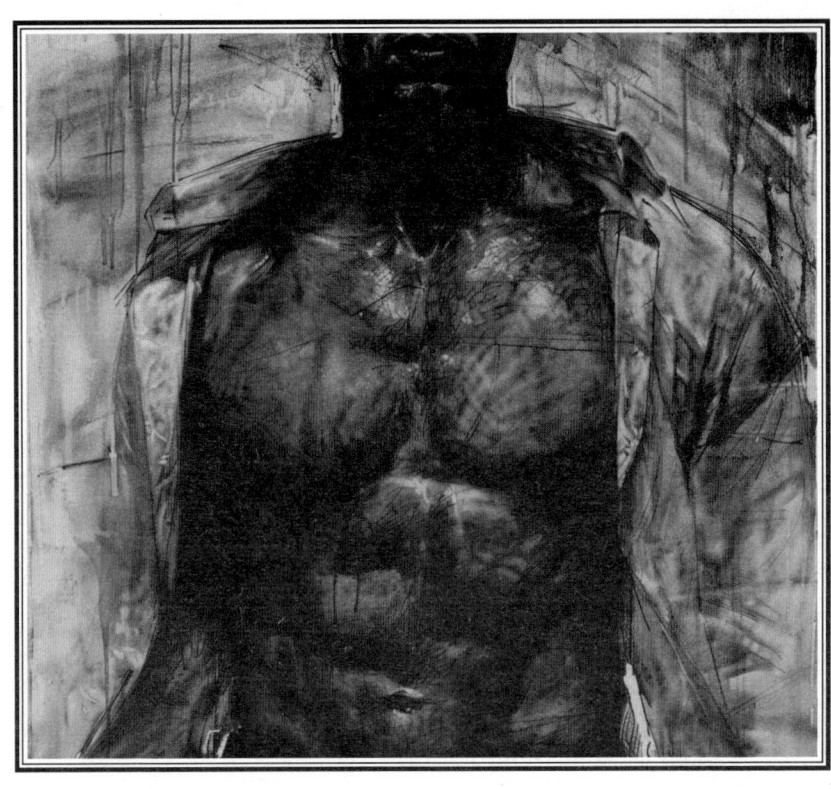

A Taxonomy of Dukes (incomplete)

very least when you see his abs. Here are some common dukes.

The Duke of X: An industrious duke of common roots, he is a ruthless man of business with a self-made fortune who was enduked later in life. His hard exterior masks a need for control born of his desire to protect those he loves.

Abs of steel from being ruthless.

The Duke of Y: A long-lost duke, rakish in his youth, lost at war or sea, whose time in the exotics becoming a real man has left him with an anachronistic tan over rippling muscles, and eyes newly cynical about the problematic inequalities of the high society into which he was born.

Abs of steel from when a problematically foreign and exotic beauty taught him about the clitoris.

The Duke of B: A seemingly trivial duke with a secret spy network and a role dashingly saving the king and country from sinister evil clubs and societies (usually the Hellfire one but sometimes something Latin or Greek). They love sacrificing virgins; he loves punching a weak-chinned lordling set on ravishment.

Abs of steel from holding all the secrets in.

The Duke of C: An uptight duke with an overactive sense of responsibility and probably a younger sister. Apparently extremely arrogant and so conscious of his position as a duke that he's willing to put you in your place about it; it turns out that also means taking his shirt off to work in the fields with his men and being on first-name terms with the villagers. Refuses to marry for love because his mum was sad, and he carries trauma about it. Will marry only for ruthlessly appropriate reasons . . . unless a chaotic beauty comes and turns his life inside out.

Abs of steel from judging matchmaking mammas, and all the field-work and common-man-handshaking.

The Duke of D: Actually a laird. No-nonsense, gruff, possible misogynist out of the gate, and unlikely to trust or understand women except for a beloved mother or sister. He's likely to have had his heart broken by a beautiful and disdainful hussy, or possibly had a first love die on him at the hands of fever or a Bad Man. Dresses poorly and is dismissive of the fripperies of mainstream English aristocracy. Lives by an older code of honour and probably has a castle that could do with some fixing up by a damsel with an eye for a home reno.

Abs of steel from riding bareback in a kilt.

The Duke of E: A slutty duke. Never compromises a maiden but will take all the merry widows or unfaithful wives that life throws at his head. Usually disillusioned about women because he was tricked by one in his youth and now is careful to stay off the marriage mart. Will either be forced by an elderly relative into agreeing to look for a bride, or used by a maiden that needs ruining to compromise herself, and must therefore fall in sexy love with an innocence that to him had previously seemed in every way repugnant.

Abs of steel from the demands of all the merry widows.

A Taxonomy of Dukes (incomplete)

The Duke of F: A tortured duke. He's guarded his heart with barriers of emotional distance to protect himself from further pain. But he has a soft spot for a woman who can make him love again through her inherent specialness. We know she is special because she makes him feel things he couldn't previously feel, and those things he feels are feelings. Or maybe her bosoms. Or both.

Abs of steel from the pain of memory or the push-ups he does to keep the pain of memory away.

Hero Jobs

On occasion, heroes are not dukes. In modern Romance they may be Cowboys, Billionaires, Bikers, Mafia Dons, Rodeo Riders, Extremely Successful in Finance or Sportsmen. It is extremely unusual for a hero to have a 9 to 5 job. The ideal job for a Romance hero leaves plenty of time for pining, for swoon-worthy antics and, ideally and most fantastically, for Never Having To Think About Money.

Romance heroines ought really to have ambitions or interests, and ideally a career path, particularly in modern Romance, but most jobs in Romance are ones that involve a lot of spare time.* Otherwise the Romance must be crammed in while on holiday, in the midst of packing up your dead grandmother's house, or while vengefully solo on the honeymoon you'd arranged with the caddish ex fiancé who cheated on you.

---

* This is not the case if our destined lovers work together, in which case it's a 24/7 job of bodyguarding, assistanting, being on a stakeout or solving a mystery.

Hero Jobs

Non-duke jobs are rarer in Historical Romance but can include Highwayman (often temporarily dispossessed of land), Owner of Gambling Club, Self-made Tycoon, Crime Boss or Highland Laird. The availability of jobs can depend on the accuracy of the historical setting, which can range from the extremely accurate to the merely gestural.* The jobs available and period faithful attitudes to both men's and women's work are potentially difficult to resolve in a way that is satisfying to lay readers, time travellers and pedantic historians. One way to avoid such issues is to write your Romance in the sweeping subgenre of Fantasy.†

---

*   Vibe-based.

†   Currently marketed as Romantasy. Fantasy allows you to mix and match social mores without triggering the more historico-accuracy-minded of your readers.

Fantasy

THE DRAGON LORD'S LADY
[Fantasy, Shifter, Assassins]

The Dragon Lord's Lady *is the fifteenth in LaGuarde's groundbreaking Fantasy Romance Thriller series with a feminist twist.*

Balentheon is a ruthless mercenary, the bastard son of the dragon king, proving himself to his estranged father by running merchant caravans through the wild desert wastes of the Blighted Quadrant. His dragon cunning serves him well in the cut-throat trade cities of Saranthablan but his human half can't help hungering for a more settled life and a maiden of his own.

Salexandra is an orphaned healer of one of the recently decimated witch tribes, travelling across the Blighted Quadrant to claim her inheritance from her aunt, The Sexy Sinister Feminist Witch Queen. Trained on spec by a wandering assassin, Salexandra was adopted by *her* witch tribe.

Fantasy

Salexandra prefers to use her skills for healing but sometimes a girl's just gotta become a whirlwind of graceful death.

When her caravan is set upon in the desert by a fanatic seeking the death of the witch queen's heir, she's the only survivor.*

Protected by her magic amulet, she's all alone in the desert with nowhere to go until Balentheon's caravan picks her up and saves her life.

Balentheon is ruthlessly reluctant to bring on a useless extra mouth in his economically viable caravan but Salexandra promises to exchange healing and assassination services for passage through the desert.

Salexandra wants to be annoyed by his mercenary ruthlessness but she's drawn to his brooding muscularity and his unusually high core temperature.

When he falls ill from a rare Blighted Quadrant fever she uncovers his dragon secret and draws him back from the brink of death with the only cure for dragon fever, which is having sex.

They should part when they reach the trade cities of Saranthablan but Balentheon's dragon self has bonded with Salexandra and he promises to protect her on her way to her feminist witch aunt.

As their burgeoning romance blossoms, Balentheon must deal with his feelings of dragon rage and bastard betrayal

---

* Which is basically the opposite of what the fanatics were going for.

A Passion for Passion

when he finds out that Salexandra is the witch queen's heir.

Will the sinister feminist witch queen ever accept such a manly dragon man as Salexandra's consort?

Who will they assassinate along the way?

How many pages can a sex scene take?

Find out in *The Dragon Lord's Lady*. Available now only by the light of the desert moon.

A Passion for Passion

THE CRYSTAL THRONE
[Fantasy, Cross-Dressing, Spiders]

Part six in the high Fantasy Romance Thriller series 'The Borders of Wingerdrom', The Crystal Throne *follows the children of Ganandanar and Draxto, who so memorably conquered the kingdom of Wingerdrom in part five, casting out the Dark Lord to his pit fortress in the dark chasm of Lovogram.**

Lark is an orphaned servant girl toiling in the kitchens of the Dark Lord's fortress. Her days are spent obeying the cruel whims of the fortress's many-legged aristocracy and her nights are spent painting beautiful artworks and doing very good archery.
    She dreams of escape . . . *but where*?!
Dermian is the rakish son of Ganandanar and Draxto. Raised on stories of battle and triumph, he longs for adventure but soothes his passionate spirit by banging lots of ladies and loving none. When his cousin Wrathena is kidnapped by servants of the Dark Lord, he follows her into Lovogram to prove his might in arms. Chased by guards and almost killed,

---

* In the 'Borders of Wingerdrom' series books one through seven, it is implied that the social hierarchy of class under the Crystal Throne is controlled by tradition and breeding, but in books eight through ten it's stated explicitly that who becomes a lord or not is determined by a lottery run by the gods and then via access to a particular chemical cocktail. D'Ancey apologises for this inconsistency and notes that for almost all of the 200 books created during the period in question, the author also had access to a particular chemical cocktail, and it may have affected the writing.

Fantasy

he finds he can't leave without the mysterious servant girl who hid him during his escape by making out with him in a sexy way at the risk of her own life. Beautiful despite her filth, and attractive to him despite her low class, Dermian will not dishonour her despite her sexiness and good archery skills, but brings her with him to his palace home.

Dragged from her lowly position in the depths of the Dark Lord's fortress and dressed in beautiful clothes that showcase her creamy breasts and fiery eyes, Lark thrills to find herself a lady in the court of Wingerdrom but she feels like an imposter until her paintings are seen by Ganandanar and Draxto, who realise she must be the daughter of their loyal minstrel/artist/painter friend Greg, who (you'll remember from the previous book) sacrificed his life to save them. Secure in her new identity she decides she will never be parted from Dermian, whom she secretly loves.

Dermian wants Lark for her creamy breasts and good personality but now he must go to war.

While at war, Dermian befriends a young archer in his legion. He is drawn to the young lad's fiery eyes and gentle spirit. They adventure together, learning respect for one another, and Lark, who is secretly in disguise as the archer, Blark, pines after the oblivious prince. It's not until her shirt is coincidentally ripped open during a fight with the Wingéd Wyverns of the Western Wastes, revealing her creamy breasts, that Dermian realises the archer he has been befriending is his left-behind love.

They must test the ancient legend that two warriors can only tame the Wingéd Wyverns by having sex.

A Passion for Passion

But will explosively sensual cross-class sex ruin their tentative cross-dressing friendship?

Will Dermian ever be able to forgive Lark for her deception or will it break the burgeoning lust and trust between them? Will the two of them tame the Wyverns and bring them back to fight for Wingerdrom? Does anyone remember Dermian's cousin from before?

Find *that* out in part seven of the high Fantasy Romance Thriller series 'The Borders of Wingerdrom' to be continued . . . *The Crystal Staff: Crystal Throne 2, Two Thrones, Too Crystalline*. Available in all good book vans and when the clock strikes three.*

---

*   Must be a grandfather clock, but in any time zone.

Fantasy

THE CRYSTAL STAFF: CRYSTAL THRONE 2, TWO THRONES, TOO CRYSTALLINE
[Fantasy, Carnie, Family Drama]

The Crystal Staff *is the next instalment of D'Ancey LaGuarde's 'Borders of Wingerdrom' series of supernatural Thrillers with an excellent twist.*

A heroine full of sassy spunk and secret longing . . . a hero full of massive muscles and also spunk . . . !

Bear is a small medium working in a large circus; she's in disguise as a simple charlatan, a comforting fortune-teller and a gardener. But her disguise disguises a deeper truth: she's actually a seer, half-social worker, half-witch.

She's a real medium disguised as a fake medium, giving people relationship advice in the guise of prophecy while ignoring her own virginity until she realises that the tall, dark stranger she keeps seeing in her crystal ball is her secret destiny, and the biggest danger . . . is to her heart!

Lonathan is tall, dark and halfling. A prince, the half-heir to a ruthless warlord, seeking to prove his own blood-thirstiness to his brutal father, and earn the Bone Throne: the throne of bone his father sits on. He is in constant internal conflict between his warring natures as half-dryad and half-warlord. His pacifist leanings and love of flowers undermine any satisfaction he might feel doing his day job of constant murder. Until one day he goes to the circus and meets Bear and his life will never be the same again.

A Passion for Passion

He's a mass murderer with a heart of gold, she's a virgin who can't ride.

Lonathan knows Bear is destined to be his kingmaker with her ability to see the future,* a skill he can use against his many awful brothers who are all trying to murder each other for their father's love. He wants her as a powerful weapon but will she instead cure the warlord's need to murder his enemies and turn him into a good man which in turn would render him weak in the face of his full-warlord half-brothers? His smouldering advances set her loins on fire but will she be able to use his spunk to put them out?

With a brief cameo by Dermian's cousin Wrathena, who escaped Lovogram and is now on the run as a cheeky yet heartless mercenary, quick with a whip and a quip, but dealing with serious abandonment issues that may or may not be setting up the next book's love interest, *The Crystal Staff* is a Romantasy that will leave you wanting more.

---

* Yes, it was heavily implied in the first 'Borders of Wingerdrom' book that the second in the series would be about Wrathena but D'Ancey tricked you. Actually, that's in the third book, *Crystal Throne 4: Tokyo Drift*.

But Why Vampires?

*Maybe it's as simple as some people just
like having their necks sucked on.*
D'ANCEY LAGUARDE

Much ink has been spilled and much blood has been metaphored in the discussion of why vampires are a) so big in culture and b) so sexy.

From the simple scientific use of vampires as a medical explanation for anaemia (why is my horny teen daughter fainting all over the place? Must be a loose man-bat!), to the sociological sexification of vampires (they always ask for consent! Hot! They penetrate you in multiple places at once! Super hot! They're cold! Hot!), vampires are a powerful place for humans to stash their fertile imagination seeds and let them grow.*

---

* Oddly enough, despite one obvious analogy for vampires in the animal kingdom being giant mosquitoes, very little fiction describes vampire

A Passion for Passion

In a world where there are few taboos against even casual one-night stands, it's difficult for a Romance author to create and build the kind of slow-burn escalating sexual tension that makes banging the ultimate expressive explosion of true love and the description of a sex climax into an emotional climax over and above the standard galactic descriptions of jizzing or lady jizzing.

For many an ambitious Romance writer, the options for making sex sexy again must therefore be either religion (forbidden love!), rivalry (forbidden lust!) or vampirism (forbidden sexy biting!).

Vampirism, and the dangers inherent in indulging in unrestrained appetite, create once more the tension and danger of a will-they-won't-they storyline, and make sexual restraint morally laudable again.

It's not very noble to take your penis from the gaming table of mutual longing in a world where sex isn't going to ruin your lover's reputation. It's just rude. *But*, if penetrating the object of his desire might turn the noble hero into a blood-crazed monster, the reader once more has skin in the game.*

---

bites as being maddeningly itchy, or suggests that vampires make a loud whining noise, which we must attribute to the early sexification of the creature-genre.

* Also, the idea of a man with hundreds of years of pent-up sexiness deciding you're the best one of all is a reward to all the secret 'pick me' longing.

But Why Half-Vampires?

Well, while we like the thrill of the possibility that our hero-lover is at risk of succumbing to his dark side, we'd also probably rather he *didn't* eat his love interest.*

The half-breed or bastard son occupies a unique social and narrative position, particularly in worlds with very rigid rules and caste systems. He is born an outsider and can operate around and without the rules that bind his peers.

Whether those rules are the magical physics that govern what each creature can do, or the rules that govern what a noble son might turn his hand to, the bastard half-breed can move in the liminal spaces, the owning of gambling clubs, the marrying outside his rank, the dark exceptions and the

---

* Yes, I know. There will always be at least some people who find almost anything romantic or sexy. That said, stories in which eating one's lover constitutes the plot are somewhat outside the realm of D'Ancey's 'Grand Oeuvre' (this is French for 'massive egg').

A Passion for Passion

dimly lit alleyways in which so much exciting rule-breaking and emotionally significant fingering can take place.

The halfie is the ultimate bad-boy. An outsider even among the most outside outsiders. He's the one for whom having a code of honour is ALSO A REBELLION AGAINST HIS DAD. Hot.

Dark and Middle Ages

A DARKLING SAIL
[Vikings, Enemies-to-Lovers]

A Darkling Sail *is a Dark Ages Romance set in the Dark Ages of the human heart.*

Thurn is the son of a Viking chieftain, a half-Viking berserker, half-slut. Tasked with guiding a ship to England's rich shores for conquest, he spends his days raiding and pillaging but it doesn't fill the hole in his heart. He's looking for a lady but he can't let himself be vulnerable, lest he reveal his terrible secret.

His Viking bloodlust hides his secret lust . . . for love!

Æthelfroth is a maiden working at a convent to escape her terrible past. Her days are spent in prayer and contemplation. When her convent is raided by Vikings, she can't forget the handsome giant who pillaged her. Captured as a slave by the brutal invaders, she wants to be angry but she can't resist the ruffianly allure of the enormous captain whose violent demeanour hides a longing for cuddles. And when she is assigned to his household she must prove that she can be more than just a captured servant.

She can be her own woman . . . and maybe his.

When the Viking village is haunted by a local witch, only Æthelfroth has the skills to take her down, and Thurn must support her independent womanhood as they uncover a network of wicked witches and dire wolves in local politics while also having sex.

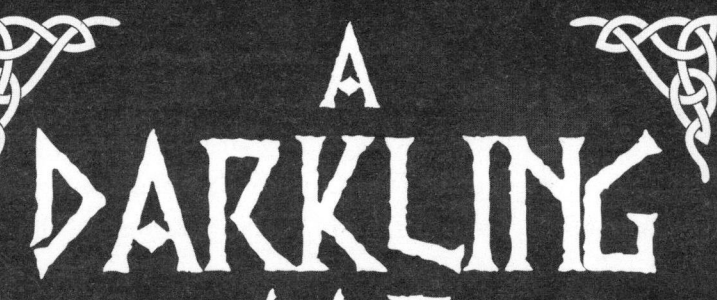

A DARKLING SAIL

He stole the virgin... ...who would steal his heart!

D'ANCEY LAGUARDE

A Passion for Passion

THE PIERCING FALCON
[Mediaeval, Epistolary, Fated Mates]

The Piercing Falcon *is a Fantasy Romance Thriller with a supernatural twist. Set in the world of Chaucer's* Canterbury Tales, *this steamy sex-fest gets right under the kirtle of a mediaeval Fantasy England, where sprites and boggarts frolic alongside dark, ancient, sexy sex-vampires. Garwin is the bastard stepson of a fae earl, a race known for their skills in* magic, music, deduction *and* seduction. *They control all human access to detectives. Those high in the fae court rarely enter the realm of humans but when they do they find work as magical detectives who can only be paid in sex. They're sextectives. They're sex-vampires who work as detectives and get paid in sex.*

Garwin, estranged from his fae stepfather and exiled from the land of the fae by the nasty curse of a hedge witch ex-lover, must roam the world as a slutty errant minstrel detective, atoning for the sins of his past and banging ladies regularly.

But no matter how many fair or noble ladies touch his penis, none of them touch his heart. He spends his days in deduction and song, riddles and mysteries, and his nights indulging his darker fae passion: his passion for sex. Until he breaks the curse he cannot take his place as a prince in the court of the fae but must spend his life in the human realm as a musician/magician/sextective solving crimes and doing spells while maintaining a career in the arts. He can only break the curse by finding true love . . . but true love is the only crime he can't solve.

Dark and Middle Ages

Gundred is the tone-deaf fourteen-year-old widow of an ageing count.

Purchased from her parents as the count's reluctant fifth bride, after the mysterious deaths in childbirth of the previous four, she is married and immediately widowed un-banged as she finds her seedy old husband promptly murdered by Viagra magic on their wedding night, leaving her virginal, wealthy, under suspicion of witchcraft and wondering how to solve a murder for which she is profoundly grateful.

When Gundred sends to good King Ethelred for help in solving the mysterious murder of her aged and hideous husband, he sends Garwin, whose price for helping her is a single chaste kiss; a kiss that sparks flames deep in her fourteen-year-old widow's heart. Even though Gundred is totally tone-deaf and therefore immune to Garwin's melodious fae sex magic, a true spark flames between her and the magical detective minstrel as they solve the mystery together.* But while the morals of the period would have found their pairing perfectly acceptable, Garwin instinctively knows that she's too young for a romance to be narratively unproblematic.

He promises to serve faithfully as her part-time knight and long-distance mentor and they exchange passionate letters via carrier pigeon as he travels from village to castle swapping songs and law enforcement for sex and different kinds of sex-related stuff.

---

* Her late husband had wrongly prepared his Viagra magic dosage by using the old king's standard spoon size not the new king's standard spoon.

A Passion for Passion

Ten years later, a supernatural crime at a masquerade ball means the two must work together to solve another crime of dark magic and darker passion and restore a priceless heirloom to Garwin's estranged stepfather the fae earl while also fighting their rising desire to consummate their dormant connection . . . by having sex!

Gundred is all grown up and has desires that Garwin can feel in his fae bones — one bone in particular.

His honour demands chaste service towards his sworn lady but Gundred and his penis demand more. Will these two mediaeval lovers untangle their crossed stars? Will Garwin open his heart as well as his pants to cure his curse? Will the hedge witch finally get her comeuppance? Will Garwin's stepfather's new wife accept the tone-deaf Gundred as her new step-stepdaughter-in-law at the musical court of the sexy fae?

Find out in *The Piercing Falcon*. Available only on vellum scroll.

EXTRACT FROM *THE PIERCING FALCON*

Ten years after the inciting incident, Garwin and Gundred reunite to solve another supernatural crime, sparking deeper desires and challenging Garwin's vow of chastity. Their love and Garwin's quest to break his curse intertwine as they face dark magic, familial estrangement and their passionate bond.[*]

---

[*] The audience has been waiting ten years for this reunion, only for the

Gundred paced the length of her chamber, her silk gown rustling with each agitated step. The flickering candlelight cast long shadows on the stone walls, adding an eerie ambiance to the room. She glanced out of the narrow window slit, watching the moonlit courtyard below, where Garwin stood, his lute slung over his muscular shoulder, conversing in low tones with the castle guards. His presence brought her both shocking satisfaction and an aching yearning she could barely contain. As a fourteen-year-old widow, she had given her heart into his keeping, barely understanding what drew her to trust him alone.

Her heart raced as she recalled his passionate letters of mentorship over the past ten years, the way his words had soothed and comforted her as she navigated her new life as a wealthy virginal teen widow in the court of the good King Ethelred after they had solved the murder of her horrible old husband together.

She had first received each letter from Garwin with the innocent longing of an infatuated adolescent; half heartbroken and half glad he was safely miles away so that she could indulge her yearning. She had pressed the letters to her mouth and breast, poring over them for hours, wishing she could read. Initially, her replies had been mainly pressed flowers and pictures of ducks until she had managed to bribe a local monk to teach her how to write.

---

narrative to plunge immediately into flashbacks.

A Passion for Passion

She had known even then that what she felt — so powerful and unformed — was something both more and less than love. What had dominated her heart then was something reminiscent of the passion a young lady might feel for her favourite member of a minstrel boy band. But now... now she had blossomed into the fullness of her femininity, her alabaster curves and ripe lips were the topic of poetry among admiring courtiers, and her shining locks and widow's freedoms the subject of envy among her female friends and rivals. Now the more mature longing she felt for his half-remembered masculinity rose in her body like the shimmering heat over a field on a summer's day if the field were on fire.

A knock at the door jolted her from her reverie. She turned to see Garwin, shadowed in the doorway, his piercing blue eyes locked onto hers, the flicker of candlelight reflecting in their fae depths.

Immediately she was cast back to the moment ten years before, the first time he had come to her room alone, midway through the investigation into her husband's death.

※

'Gundred,' he said, his voice a velvet caress. 'I believe we may have a lead on your husband's murder. But we must tread carefully.'

She swallowed hard, her adolescent pulse quickening. 'What have you discovered?'

Garwin stepped closer, his scent — a heady mix of

forest and magic – enveloping her. 'The potion that killed your husband... it was no ordinary Viagra magic. It was brewed by someone with deep knowledge of the fae arts. Someone with a personal vendetta.'

Gundred's breath hitched. 'The hedge witch?'

He nodded, his gaze intense. 'Aye. But there's more. She was brought the poison recipe by someone. The heirloom stolen from my stepfather's court holds the key to unravelling this mystery. We must retrieve it to break the curse that binds us both.'

As he spoke, Gundred felt an overwhelming urge to reach out, to touch him, to feel the warmth of his skin beneath her fingers. She took a step closer, her voice trembling. 'Garwin, we must find this heirloom. But... how can I resist what I feel for you?'

Garwin's eyes darkened. 'Gundred, my honour binds me to serve you chastely, and at more than 400 years old, soul bonded though we are, making out with a teenager would just feel a bit... wrong.' He reached out, gently tucking a lock of her hair behind her ear. His touch sent a shiver down her spine.

'Many women are married at my age, and bearing children not much older,' she whispered, persuasively.

'Yes,' he murmured, 'but I just can't help feeling that in ages to come, people might not look so kindly on a 386-year age difference, particularly when you still haven't finished developing your prefrontal cortex.' He rested one cool hand on her hot forehead, as though testing for the fever that she felt raging through her blood.

'Then let us make a vow,' she whispered, her voice barely audible. 'To solve this murder and reclaim your place in the fae court. And once we have, and I have finished developing my prefrontal cortex to the extent that it wouldn't be icky, we will allow ourselves to be together fully, without reservation.'

Garwin's hand cupped her cheek, his thumb tracing the curve of her lips. 'A vow, then,' he murmured, his lips hovering inches from her vibrating forehead. 'To honour and protect, to solve this mystery . . . and, when it is no longer deeply problematic, to finally give in to the passion that binds us.'

Their breath mingled, the tension between them palpable. But even as his lips brushed her forehead in a chaste promise of what was to come, they both knew their hearts and destinies were entwined far deeper than mere vows. This was a love forged in magic and mystery, and nothing – not even the darkest of curses – could keep them apart for long.

※

Ten years later and here he was, standing in her doorway, a long, tall goblet of mead, the light sparking shards from his icy eyes directly into her heated heart. The steam that rose from the sudden mixture of hot and cold somehow also filled her underskirts with a simmering warmth . . .

Creatures: Werewolves

THE MASTER-LAIRD'S WOLF-LORD
[Historical, BDSM, LGBTQ+]

This supernatural Thriller is a classic werewolf-meets-vampire-meets-BDSM story.

He is Mac McKinley, a Highlander-cum-cum-vampire, enslaved for years by a sinister clan of vampire-vampires.*

After escaping years of torture† from the vampire horde,

---

* Vampires who feed on vampires. This is not as self-explanatory as you'd think; vampire-vampires arose from needy Gothic teens who, hanging round graveyards too much, eventually figured out that you could suck the life out of a vampire just by hitting on them aggressively enough for long enough.

† Lots of asking if this batwing shirt from Hot Topic makes them look hotly undead or un-hotly undead.

A Passion for Passion

he meets his match in Sakino, half-Samurai, half-werewolf and count of the ancient Roman werewolf court.* Mac McKinley is in no mood to fall in love . . . until he does.†

Accompanied by his sidekick and adopted sister Sandra, a small, sassy, ethereal half-Valkyrie, half-werewolf, who will definitely get a spin-off book,‡ the tormented laird is captured

---

*   Some cruel commentators have suggested that the ancient Romans did not have a Samurai tradition. To which D'Ancey has always responded that to assume ancient Roman werewolves were not internationally well travelled is racist. (It is unclear whether we are to infer this response as meaning objectors are being racist against werewolves, Italians or Japanese people.)

†   The opening sequences of the book, in which we see McKinley roaming his Scottish lands, coexisting peacefully within a feudal symbiosis, are beyond idyllic and caused a surge in tourism to the Scottish Highlands, a phenomenon which was repeated by D'Ancey novels over time and has led the Scottish government at various times to attempt to suppress publications in order to preserve basic infrastructure.

   It's said that one of the reasons the annual Edinburgh Festival Fringe is so prohibitively expensive to artists and audiences is D'Ancey's lustful description of McKinley splayed artfully across a rock formation at the top of Arthur's Seat, a local landmark, fingering Arthur, a local maiden.

   The literary significance of the sequence has been debated, with some suggesting this means that McKinley is closeted at the outset of the text, others that McKinley is bisexual. D'Ancey, on being asked, shrugged and said, 'What can I say, the laird likes fingering'; a typically enigmatic answer.

‡   Sandra is often depicted in art as wearing the classically anachronistic double-horned helmet falsely attributed to the Vikings. Of course in real life, this would not have left room for her wolfy ears, and she is more likely to have worn a Kevlar-hardened gravity-defying hairstyle like 80s comic-book X-Man Storm's mohawk, but more so and with metal for deadly headbutting.

once more, ruthlessly but somehow way less traumatically by the count Sakino, who somehow begins to soothe the fury that is raging within him.* Among other things, a consistently shirtless Sakino immediately gets on in a platonic way with Sandra, and their sassy banter proves that Sakino can't be truly evil.

Yet, when an ancient evil from their past resurfaces, placing Mac McKinley's traditional birthright at risk, will their desire deepen into a love that can bring a proud warrior to his knees?†

Available now from all online stockists and disused phone boxes.

---

* The scene in which Sakino alternately plays McKinley music and challenges him to wrestling-chess is considered a groundbreakingly intellectual depiction of musical flirtation-cum-wrestling, and the first homoerotic description of an ancient Roman werewolf lord being aggressively castled.

† Yes.

Creatures: Werewolves

LITTLE RED RIDING WEREWOLF
[Fairy Tale, Fantasy, Werewolf]

Little Red Riding Werewolf *is a dark Romance Thriller with a supernatural twist, a sexy sequel to the famous fairy tale.* Little Red Riding Werewolf *is the fourth in D'Ancey LaGuarde's series of fairy tale sexy remixes, 'Happily Ever After Comes Twice'.*

Gil is a buxom beauty with auburn locks who won't be told what to do. Half-werewolf, half-granddaughter, she's the dangerous offspring between a big bad wolf and his beloved riding-hood-wearing witch. Gil spends her days gathering herbs in the forest and her nights as an exotic dancer at a werewolf bar in the mediaeval-ish village of Wolfinton. She's protected by her pack of highwayman werewolves who seek to preserve her innocence in this dangerous world, but her free spirit calls for adventure.

Told to stay in the woods lest she stray into the path of one of the wolves' natural woodsman enemies, Gil rebels and heads to the nearest lumberjack station. Caught in a wood-valanche, she is trapped under a pile of wood, until she is rescued by Jack the lumberjack, whom she immediately recognises as her destined mate. Jack is struck by the beauty of the demand-avoidant redhead with the mysterious eyes and the musky wolfish scent and they impulsively kiss, unwittingly activating a life bond that can never be broken!

They must consummate their connection within fourteen days or they will both explode!

Gil demands a proper courtship and love before she is

mounted by her fated mate, but as they explore their deepening connection up against some trees, Gil's tribe discovers them in all-but-flagrante and realises that Jack is of the tribe of woods-men* who killed her grandfather the wolf. Parted by force, Jack is caged by the wolf pack in the basement of the werewolf bar in Wolfinton. They are to be reunited at the full moon, in a fortnight's time, when Jack will be staked out for Gil's wolf to eat.

Will she accidentally eat her fated mate in a blood frenzy?! Will they both explode from the expiry of their unconsummated mate-bond? Or will they have aggressive wolf sex under the pervert moon?

They must escape for the Unspeakable Mountain and make their home among the outcasts and misfits of the Forbidden Zone.

Jack and Gil must make it up the hill into a place they can call home.

---

*   Non-gender specific tribal designation.

Creatures: Werewolves

A WEEKEND WITH THE WOLF
[Post-Apocalyptic, Fairy Tale]

A Weekend with the Wolf *is the fifty-third in LaGuarde's post-apocalyptic werewolf sex-fest 'Packing It In'.**

In a post-nuclear wasteland, packs of werewolves roam the borderlands, dominating the feeble humans with their aristocratic predations, elaborate caste system and lustful slaverings. When a young woman is wed, she must first be given to the Wolf Lord of the land to whom her village belongs, in the traditional month-long *droit du seigneur*/sex month known as being thrown to the sexy wolves. Of course, wealthy human women can buy their way out of this sexy rite of passage by paying for destitute young women to be thrown to the wolves in their place.

Forbidden to marry their own kind until they attain Alpha-status, the lustful Wolf Lords must slake their hunger on innocent human maidens, whom they seduce on their wedding nights using their powerful pheromones and then return to their villages unharmed.† But young Lord Lucius

---

* Postapocalyptic mediaevelism is a great Romantasy setting because the author can create a world with exactly as many social mores as will help the plot. You can have an honour culture *and* running water. Other subgrenres of Romance in which you get out of jail free regarding historical attitudes existing alongside modern vibes include Mafia Romance, Biker Romance and Small Town Christmas Romance.

† Yet ruined for normal men by virtue of werewolves' sixth 'g-spot' sense and cultural respect for the female orgasm.

refuses to deflower the local peasantry, longing instead for the tender touch of the red-haired, city-dwelling young woman who saved him when he was caught in an urban wolf trap when he was travelling as a young wereman, and who accepted only a gentle and meaningful kiss in return for her help.

Raised on the streets of a decrepit post-apocalyptic New York, Maryann has seen her share of horrors. A scrappy survivor, she's fought for her life since she was orphaned as a child, but she's never known real fear until she's captured by a gang of girl-hunters and sent to the countryside as a sacrifice to the Wolf Lord.

Now the only thing saving her from the desecration of the wolf is Lucius's self-control. But as they spend the allotted month together, passionately just about avoiding having sex,[*] she realises that rather than revulsion, she craves his lupine lust.

As the final full moon approaches, Maryann is confronted with the growing knowledge that, by denying his massive erection, Lucius is putting his own power in the pack at risk. They must work together, hand-in-paw, to overcome the age-old battle between their people and forge a new future where humans and half-humans/half-wolves can live in sexy harmony.

---

[*] Second base, but *very* second base.

But Why Werewolves?

> *Well, we all know some people who are just dog people.*
> D'ANCEY LAGUARDE

When we ask ourselves why werewolves fire the groin of the narrative mind, it's easy to think 'Well, all Romance is wish fulfilment of some sort, maybe women just want a man who understands the stresses and pressures of having a monthly cycle.'

But of course, everything is always more than one thing.* A werewolf is a man who is fully aware of and in communication with his animal self; inherently violent and physically dominant, his gentleness with a mate is therefore an act of strength rather than an act of weakness. Also, often they'll come with a pack, and isn't it nice to imagine being with someone who has friends and an active social group, whether

---

* Usually it's at least a metaphor for something else.

A Passion for Passion

that's a regular board games night or scrapping for status in a dog hierarchy and howling at the moon with the boys.

Have we not all looked at someone doing romance by the book and thought, are they being nice because they *have to*? What is more powerfully sexy than someone who *could* turn into a giant wolf and eat your ribs but *chooses* not to?

Leopard Shifters

*Leopard-shifter heroes are perfect for people
who think cats are sexier than dogs.*
D'ANCEY LAGUARDE

NIGHT PASSIONS
[Leopard Shifter, Fight-Club Romance]

Night Passions *is a highly charged erotic Thriller set in the mean streets of DownTown where life is cheap and beer is expensive (but still obviously cheaper than life, which seems reasonable).*

Sebastian Church is a changeling. Born of an unnatural threesome at a satanic 70s swinger night, he is part-leopard, part-human, part-undercover cop and all hunk.

He keeps his animalistic urges under tight control in his day job as a highly paid corporate psychoanalyst, but he can't keep denying the call to dance music and gratuitous violence in his blood and he spends his nights as the star attraction in a supernatural fight club/nightclub.

A Passion for Passion

Brunella is a part-time medium working night shifts on the door of the supernatural fight club/nightclub to support her big dream of becoming a full-time medium, but when she has a dusk vision of match-fixing in the club, she finds herself asking for help from the tall, dark stranger whose aura she can't read.

As Sebastian and Brunella are drawn into a web of intrigue and night fights, they must solve the crime together and uncover the sinister undercover fight club match-fixing cabal . . . while also having sex.

Will Brunella ever be able to trust a man who is part-leopard when she is deathly allergic to cats?*

And can a medium with cat allergies and a leopard-cop-hunk-psychoanalyst-gladiator ever make it work?

'The most graphic description of a leopard's penis we've ever seen' – *Guardian*

'The second most graphic description of a leopard's penis we've ever seen'† – *The Times*

Night Passions is available now in all airports and under bus stop benches. Buy it now and enter the night.

---

* The scene where Sebastian buys antihistamines and condoms for Brunella at the chemist is often held up as a groundbreaking moment for the genre of Romance novels, which had hitherto mostly avoided dealing with the logistics of consent and sexual preparation. That the buying of the antihistamines is a deeply vulnerable and emotional moment for Sebastian is only a bonus for fans of the pairing.

† When asked for a statement, *The Times* refused to disclose the first most graphic description of a leopard's penis they'd ever seen.

A Passion for Passion

LIGHT FINGERS IN DARKNESS
[Crime, Hurt-Comfort, Leopard Shifter with PTSD]

Light Fingers in Darkness *is the first in LaGuarde's 'Shapeshifters and Shoplifters' series of modern detective Romance Thrillers with a supernatural twist.*

Legacy is a changeling leopard-shifter male brought up in an orphan pickpocket gang, now a self-made billionaire on the hunt for a mate while dealing with the dark past that has locked his shapeshifting powers away from him. He can only change when he is in moments of extreme anger or lust. And that's not always appropriate.*

Lara is a part-time bartender, part-time biochemist, part-time detective who can't stop thinking about the quiet billionaire who drinks alone at her bar. She wants to hear his secrets and soothe his pain but she must struggle against her fear of billionaires from her first abusive billionaire boyfriend. **She's afraid of making herself vulnerable to love and money. He's afraid of accidentally turning into a leopard and eating her in her sleep.**

Legacy wants Lara just as much as she wants him but he doesn't want to hurt her feelings by accidentally murdering her in a fit of leopardism.

---

* You might ask exactly when turning into a 9-feet-tall leopard man with a badge and an erection would be appropriate and I would answer that the very question reveals your imagination was not distorted by unregulated adolescent access to online fan fiction.

Leopard Shifters

Lara must use her biochemistry skills to solve the secrets that lie in Legacy's blood and figure out how she can tame his inner beast. As heat simmers between them, they must restrict themselves to mutual fingering while they solve the mystery of who locked Legacy's power away from him and why it was Lara's abusive billionaire ex-boyfriend.

Together, they must work through the passion that is rising between them if they are to have any chance of forever.

But Why Sexiness?

In an action movie, an action sequence should move the plot forward; it should be an expression or exploration of the characters. If everyone punches the same, there's no point in punching at all. So it is with musicals; if a song doesn't reveal something new about a character or relationship, you might as well save the money on choreography and just have it be a play. Likewise in Romance, sex. Every time a character is fingered on a horse, it should be a unique and relationship-building event.

That's because the point of Romance as a genre isn't that the characters have sex, though it might be a significant part of the plot. In a good action movie, the punching *gets us somewhere*: defeats our enemies, removes obstacles, demonstrates when a character has overcome their fears. Like in *Die Hard*, where the character of Bruce Willis's radio-contact/police friend is afraid to use his gun because he accidentally killed a child and then at the end of the movie he gains the confidence to murder again.*

The point is, Romance tells stories about relationships, and sexiness, whether explicitly explored or tastefully implied behind a fluttering curtain, is a significant part of the story of many relationships.

One handy thing about Romance novels is that the sex, being more or less part of the plot, can be both sexy in itself and also function as a narrative device to further the romance that is the main story. Competent horseback fingering functions in a Romance plot as the murdering-a-man-with-a-pencil sequence functions in an action movie: to explore character and drive motivation.

The idea that sex should be or can be *romantic* is often characterised as naïve, old-fashioned, girly or somehow prudish. The implication being that modern and enlightened people are satisfied with physical pleasure in itself, stripped of the illusions and delusions and pressures of longform narrative arcs. The vibe of such critique is that if you are the kind of people who believe romance and connection might improve sex, you're suggesting that actually it *redeems* sex in a vaguely religious values kind of way, and to imply that sex ought to be romantic is sort of downgrading the validity of the pleasure of sex qua sex.

---

* This character arc doesn't stand up so well as a victorious moment in the light of modern politics, but it was an extremely moving moment of triumph for the character in more innocent times when we approved of police violence.

But Romance is unashamed to value the romantic, with sex being either in service to or in conflict with the essential goal of the narrative, which is that by the end the leading characters ought to get to a point where we can believe in an ever after that is sustainably happy.

The place of sexiness in Romance is always at least a bit political, though ideally not overtly political because actual politics are inherently gonad-shrivelling. While lots of sex in Romance, particularly Romances written in the historical period known as 'back in the day', is what would be described now as 'problematic', it's always been a little bit groundbreaking as well.

Describing sex where a woman's point of view and pleasure is the primary focus has always been a bit revolutionary, even in periods of time where the story of sexiness in Romance novels was just that the hero had a magic penis, and penetration was sufficient to cause waves of inconceivable ecstasy. This was because in various periods of mainstream cultural sex politics, even in the wildest fantasies, a man who knew how to find a clitoris and was willing to do so was beyond the scope of imagination.*

---

* To put that in perspective, many Romance authors in the 80s *could not* imagine a competent lover who — even seized with irresistible passion to claim his beloved — might prioritise foreplay, but *could easily* imagine a noble duke returning from a voyage in which his father had been murdered with a crocodile at the hands of an evil viscount, and *then* imagine that grieving son disguising himself as a pirate in order to reclaim his lost inheritance from (and only from) the corrupt viscount's trading vessels and *then* imagine that fake pirate accidentally kidnapping a spoiled heiress with a palpitating bust and a penchant for trying to escape while partially clad on a small boat in the middle of the ocean.

Whither Hotness?

You may have noticed a trend in modern storytelling, particularly in the real blockbuster movies, to create stories that are further and further away from the dangerously divisive shoals of sex. In the pursuit of relatability, they have become bland. All love is about risk, all relationships have power dynamics, love is a problem. Much as a comedian seeking relatability might look for the blandest topic, and so fail to connect with anyone – 'what's the deal with airline food?'* – an aromantic story with a glossy, anodyne, egalitarian 'couple-lite' pairing in the lead theoretically makes space for everyone and misses feeling like home for anyone.

---

* The deal with airline food is that they have to prepare and transport a huge quantity of reheatable food in a vessel that has both weight and size restrictions. More, your tastebuds change at altitude so the fact that you get anything even vaguely palatable is a miracle of both food science and engineering.

A Passion for Passion

So as superheroes and stars become ever more beautiful and ever less fuckable,* Romance novels are one of the last big holdouts of sensual sexiness. Romance novels, like *actual* sex, are about how you *feel* (while being fingered on horseback or ravished in a cupboard) rather than how you look while doing it. Real falling in love is messy, personal, sometimes problematic, deeply compromised, profoundly specific, deeply embarrassing, and it *feels like something* we recognise, whether it's in our milieu or our language or our gender preference or not. It's also a lot more relatable to the average person than backflipping through a fiftieth-storey window into a controlled wingsuit dive.

Perhaps that is why D'Ancey wrote a Romance set fully in the wet world of the Octopus People.

---

* See essay 'Everyone is Beautiful and No One is Horny' by RS Benedict, bloodknife.com/everyone-beautiful-no-one-horny

But Why Underwater Creatures?

The ocean is a sexy place. Deep, sensual, mysterious, it can play come-hither waving games, penetrate almost anything and also be full of whales banging.*

Octopuses are the closest thing we have to aliens, prancing around the seafloor, and nobody who has ever been exposed to a particular sub-subgenre of Japanese animation can deny their inherent sensual qualities. That the sexiness of octopuses is in part fuelled by national censorship laws that said you couldn't show penises is a beautiful ode to the triumph of the horny human spirit.

The idea that a rule about not showing graphic pictures of penises prompted artists to respond 'what's the animal most made of penises?' brings a thrill of joy to my heart. A surge of inspiration not unlike the thrill with which science educators talk about the journey of man to the moon.

---

* In real life, water is almost always a bad place to get it on, which gives imaginary water an additional forbidden fruitiness.

A Passion for Passion

It's not just octopuses either! Other sexy creatures lurking in the wet include whales, otters, mermaids, selkies and dugongs.*

Also, wetness is sexy and don't let anyone tell you otherwise. The sexiness of wetness, and vice versa the inherent wetness of sex, is why feather boas are not sexy.†

---

* As the great Josh Gondelman once said of sailors looking at manatees, 'I don't know what that fish is, but I'm going to fuck it.'

† D'Ancey has a very open mind about the range of things that can be considered sexy, from sentient hillocks to Isambard Kingdom Brunel. That range does not include feather boas in any form. When asked why not feather boas, D'Ancey responds with a shudder and the one word 'clagginess', which must be sufficient for our purposes if we imagine the recipe involved.

Underwater

THE MANTLE OF THE DEEP
[Experimental, Octopus-to-Lover]

First in a series of new supernatural Romance Thrillers marketed directly to the mysterious Octopus tribespeople of New New Zealand, The Mantle of the Deep *is a story of love, passion, secrets and octopus sex.*

Prince <gurgling noise> is seeking redemption after being cast out by his father, King <wave noise> of the Western Reachers. Half-octopus prince, half-vampire fish, he wanders the cold currents of the border of the Marianas Darklands, the trench that Poseidon walled off so many centuries ago to keep demon fish from emerging out of the depths. His mighty tentacles and tanned mantle hide a wounded heart.

<dripping/pouring noise> is an orphaned Megaleledonidae octopus, feeding her 3,000 sisters by hunting in the forbidden trench waters.

Her lean hunger and scrappy temper hide a passionate

beauty, a strain of magic waiting to be awakened and a creamy breast.

When Prince <gurgling noise> falls victim to an evil trench magician, only <dripping/pouring noise> volunteers to rescue him, and the moment they meet a passion rises between them that cannot be denied. But Prince <gurgling noise> cannot bring himself to disclose his dark secret. His vampire-fish heritage means he longs for fish-blood, and once he mates, it will be for life.

Will King <wave noise> accept his disgraced son back in the onshore branch of the Octopus People tribe? Can their tentacles entwine forever or will they be ripped apart by the cold currents of the heartless ocean? They must fight for their love against tide, time and the evil trench magician seeking his revenge?

The *Guardian* called *The Mantle of the Deep* 'the most educational discussion of octopus reproduction since *Legs Beneath the Waves*'.

The Times condemned it for graphic descriptions in the scene where Prince <gurgling noise> uses his specially adapted tentacle to deliver a bundle of sperm directly into <dripping/pouring noise>'s mantle cavity while they also have normal human sex.

The Mantle of the Deep is available now at the dunes on all high tides.

Underwater

A VETERAN'S HONOUR
[Selkie]

A Veteran's Honour *is the fourth in LaGuarde's 'Home-Brewed Heroes' series of Romantic Comedies with a supernatural twist.*

He's a veteran marine, she's a veterinary assistant at SeaWorld with a charming habit of falling down on the job.* She knows how to handle seals but the human heart is even more slippery and unpredictable and can't be bribed with seafood.† He's a muscular man with dreamy eyes and complex PTSD. She's a woman in a wetsuit with a pocket full of fish.

Max has returned to his extremely middle-American hometown after lots of being in the army with one aim: to look after his heroically deployed best friend's little sister in a totally platonic way. He's supposed to protect her, not fall in love with her, only she isn't his best friend's annoying little sister anymore, she's all grown up and wearing neoprene.

Tiffany is perfectly happy working at SeaWorld, concealing the fact that her public role as seal-training veterinary assistant conceals her half-selkie heritage (on her deadbeat seal-dad's side), but she needs a date to the annual SeaWorld convention and Max is right there.

---

* In Romantic Comedies, all heroines have mild dyspraxia or an inner ear infection that throws off their balance, particularly in high-stakes moments where they need to impress their boss.

† Let the marketing departments of Oyster and Lobster dinners take note.

A Passion for Passion

Every guy knows you don't hit on your best friend's little sister, no matter how strong the attraction, even when you've agreed to pose as her boyfriend at a SeaWorld event.

Tiffany and Max dive into their attraction as the metaphorical sharks are circling and also literal sharks. So when he's infected by the bite of a jealous were-merman whose hopeless unrequited passion for Tiffany has driven him mad, Tiffany and Max are drawn into the mafia currents of an underwater underworld and their fake relationship starts to feel real. They're caught in a sexy paradox. They have to convince the villains of the deep that their passion (which is real but they're both pretending isn't real) *is* real or they'll both be sleeping with the fishes . . . forever.

Underwater

KING OF THE GLOOM
[Mythology, Mermaids, Mystery]

King of the Gloom *is number seven in D'Ancey LaGuarde's modern 'Getting It on in the Pantheon: Myths and Make-outs' series of Romance Thrillers with a super-supernatural twist.*

Dananon is five hundred years old, Lucinda is eighteen. He's an immortal warrior, she's an intern at a landscape-designing franchise with a secret passion for the harp. He's the bastard son of a demigoddess and a male sea witch: half-man, half-demigod[*] heir to the kingdom of Night. They meet one night when Lucinda, playing harp in the park, is set upon by a gang of feral highwaypersons.[†]

Dananon is wounded, pierced by an iron blade, in the process of rescuing her and she must nurse him back to health. What can a half-man, quarter-god, quarter-sea wizard, all-hunk have in common with a simple apprentice landscape designer/virtuoso harpist?

But Dananon must break it to Lucinda that the moment he saw her he knew she was to be his destined mate, connected forever. He must awaken her immortal blood in the only way he knows how – with his penis.

Lucinda and Dananon are forced to develop an uneasy

---

[*] So like a quarter-god.

[†] A very open-minded gang. Just because you're a gang of feral urchins doesn't mean you have to be mean.

respect for each other as they solve a rash of underworld landscaping crimes and discover the secret identity of the Mulch Lord while they fight the sexual tension rising between them by arguing about their vast cultural differences.

But they can't resist the effulgent pheremonal magnetism of fated mateship and they resolve all of their arguments with the fiery passion of sudden sex scenes. When Dananon reveals the truth Lucinda wrestles with the fact that she's eternally bonded to a sexy near-stranger while uncovering nefarious doings at her landscape design firm.

Dananon must learn and grow into respecting her individuality as a modern empowered woman and harpist. Lucinda refuses his sexy offer of immortality until her sassy housemate, Isabella Kingdom Brunel – a super wisecracking descendant of the legendary railway designer Isambard Kingdom Brunel and heir to the Kingdom Brunel railway empire – gives her some sage advice about how hot he is before pairing up with Dananon's merman secretary.

Underwater

THE WET ONES
[Underwater, Accountancy]

After witnessing the murder of his mother by a mermaid, half-vampire elf lord, half-accountant Prince Bloodmaths[*] makes a deal with the sinister elven vampire council[†] to sate his need for statistically meaningful vengeance.[‡]

He'll catch the mermaid who did the deed but he'll pay for it with his crown, his position as Accounting Officer of the Institute of Unchartered Accountants (Undead Fae Division) and his heart.

Millie, Wet Princess of Atlantis, has been told all through her childhood of the cruelty of the forbidden drylands but had never expected to encounter it first hand. Captured by Bloodmaths, the halfling prince with murder in his eyes and numbers in his blood, she fears she will soon find out! She knows (and he says) that the cruel prince will make sure she learns the worst of elven vampire-kind, but she is surprised by his gentle hands and consideration and general pro-consent attitude throughout the whole prisoner-taking process. She

---

[*] A title specific to vampires who are royal by blood and accountants by training.

[†] They're all left-handed. Also evil, but that's by coincidence.

[‡] Briefly distracted by trying to discover the optimum temperature to serve cold revenge (sub-zero? temperate-climate room temperature? gazpacho?), Prince-Count Bloodmaths eventually determined that the temperature of the revenge doesn't matter quite so much as his ability to put the conclusive outcome into a persuasive and graphic infographic.

finds her steely determination to suffer in silence undermined by his strong, cold abs and chivalric willingness to share a Sudoku puzzle with her while casting her into a surprisingly well-furnished oubliette-cum-studio apartment.

On Bloodmaths' side of the balance sheet, his honour knows he should kill her, but his heart and penis disagree – a calculation of two-thirds against that leaves him divided between vengeance and the need to bang.

He is tormented by finding his moist prisoner too appealing to torture and decides that the only ethical way to extract information is with his penis. By seducing her into revealing his mother's murderer, he will be able to complete his mission and get rid of this pesky lust that is starting to cloud his calculations.

The rules of the land and sea are changing, secrets of the past are spilling, Excel spreadsheets are getting out of control. Whether they live or die, nothing in the realm will ever be the same.

Underwater

UPSIDE-DOWN SEX
[Octopus]

Daniel is a successful banker on Wall Street.* He left his tormented history and cruel ex-fiancée behind, and by rejecting the underworld community of his youth, he believes he has left the social taint of his half-breed status as a half-demon, half-Silicon Valley startup bro with a social media platform in his past.† Everything is going Daniel's way except for one small problem: his insatiable lust for souls to eat‡ and the mysterious half-woman, half-octopus who has just crashed through his ceiling and is turning his life and his heart upside down.

OK, that's two problems.

Ariallana is out of her depth and up in the air. Escaping the indentured life of a performing songstress in an aquarium jazz bar, she was on her way out of town when, cornered by a pool shark, she leapt eight storeys up into the air vent of a residential apartment and concealed herself in what she

---

* Daniel's job provides a tantalising clue as to the publication date of this text. Wall Street heroes fell out of favour in mainstream Romance in the mid-twenty-teens, as increasingly mainstream scepticism about the goodwill of corporate entities permeated the minds and panties even of middle- and upper-class readers. That said, D'Ancey's relentless contrarianism in the face of market demand undermines the certainty of even our most confident guesses.

† The demons have *some* standards.

‡ Exponential market curves don't happen all on their own.

Upside-Down Sex

*Out of her depth,
out of water...
and in his arms*

D'Ancey LaGuarde

thought was a structurally sound ventilation cavity. Caught in the buff arms of Daniel, she thinks only of escape until suddenly the sub-brains in her additional arms inform her that he is her fated mate, without whom she will surely die.

A fish out of water, suddenly tipped into the dry upper crust of the human world, she must learn what it is to love on land, and somehow crack the shell of a man/demon/startup bro who insists his heart is harder than the heart of the ocean (the jewel in the movie about the *Titanic*).*

Daniel's comfortable assumption that his new aspirational life as a corporate sociopath would be untroubled by emotions or many-limbed women clambering lithe and moist into his arms will be shattered by their passionate connection. After years running from his past, he'll have to confront his heritage. He will have to reconcile the half of him that's a startup bro with the urge to deoptimise the time he spends with Ariallana, and how will he win the heart of a woman octopus with a mind of her own?

Why can't he stop thinking about her when he's trading on the stock market floor?†

Can she predict the football scores?‡

---

* He got his advice about masculinity from a podcast.

† Part of the reason is that people keep ordering seaweed salad for lunch and the mnemonic association of scent is making him horny.

‡ This seems at first glance to be a reference to Paul the Octopus, a common octopus who in an early viral moment in October 2010 was said to have predicted the results of international association football matches during what we can only assume was an incredibly slow news period. But, for

A Passion for Passion

Daniel must decide whether to continue with his comfortable financial trading life or to trade his future for a future with her. A pulsating tale from the author who brought you *The Lust Train* and *The Woolworths Catalogue: After Dark Edition*.

---

interdimensional literature scholars, it is worth noting that there was no such psychic octopus event in the universe in which D'Ancey LaGuarde wrote. It's possible D'Ancey just enjoyed the idea of a creature with many feet being interested in football.

America
[Modern]

A KNIGHT OF PASSION
[Mafia, Werewolves, Modern]

A Knight of Passion is book 1.8 of 'The Night Clock Patrol' series of modern detective Romance Thrillers with a supernatural twist.

Meet Callie. They call her The Bitch because she's half-detective, half-werewolf and all-bitch. Callie wears a leather jacket, with her flaming locks of auburn hair, her tiny waist and her old-fashioned creamy voluptuousness offsetting her edgy modern coolness. She's a sassy rebel and she doesn't care who knows it. Despite her famed bitchiness, she's endlessly loyal to her friends and spends most of the book doing things that are nice even though everyone says she's a bitch.

Until she meets her new detecting partner, Marcus,

recently retired from a job bodyguarding the most famous mafia were-lords.*

He's fucking massive and has a perfect body and she first meets him while he's reading a book with his hair falling over his noble brow.

But he's haunted by his dark past and is very rude to her at the same time as being hot. He's the careful one, with his military rigidity and massive torso, and his masculine protectiveness offends Callie's independent bitch spirit. He's also a werewolf, but a different kind that means *tension between them* and an age-old rivalry that expresses itself mainly in simmering sexual tension.

They say sassy things to each other while saving each other's taut butts from life-or-death situations. Callie spends a lot of time saying, 'Ugh, men.' Marcus rolls his golden eyes and polishes his guns.

It's not until they accidentally get nude in the course of a mission together that she sees his terrible sexy scars from his time in the military and understands that she's not the only person hiding her wounds. But just as Marcus hears Callie defending him to their boss and asks her on a date, a dark force arises, explaining the string of unexplained murders they'd been sexily working on together.

Callie is kidnapped and Marcus has to rescue her but then vice versa because of feminism.

Wounded and sexy, they recuperate together in Callie's

---

* Powerful men who, on the full moon, become inbred landowners.

expensive flat that she inherited from her rich grandmother, slowly building up their strength by eating chicken soup and their sexy tension by accidentally seeing each other coming out of the shower or waking up nude from a nightmare, until they join themselves in a conflagration of extreme lust and perhaps even . . . love.

The *Guardian* called *A Knight of Passion* 'an almost astonishing idea of how people interact'.

The *Washington Post* called it 'a triumph of towels'.

A Knight of Passion is available now in the back container of all motorcycles.

EXTRACT FROM *A KNIGHT OF PASSION*

Callie and Marcus find themselves in the aftermath of a harrowing encounter with the werewolf biker gang. Bruised and battered, they seek refuge in the solitude of their temporary sanctuary, yet the tension between them crackles like lightning in the charged atmosphere. Despite the adrenaline still coursing through their veins, the energy between them threatens to overpower their senses any moment.

In the dimly lit motel room, the air thick with the scent of sweat and motorbike lube, Callie's heart still raced from the adrenaline surge of their encounter with the third most menacing werewolf biker gang in Chicago.

She paced the cramped space, frustration knotting her brow as she shot a pointed look at Marcus, who leaned casually against the wall. His muscular frame seemed to fill the room, his golden eyes fixed on her with an intensity that made her pulse quicken.

'You know, Marcus,' she began, her voice laced with sarcasm, 'for a guy with muscles the size of Shrek's, you sure know how to attract trouble.'

Marcus's lips quirked into a half-smile, a hint of amusement dancing in his argent gaze as he pushed himself off the wall and stepped closer. 'And yet here you are, Callie, dragging me into your chaotic adventures once again,' he replied, his voice deep and resonant, sending a shiver down her spine. 'And do you mean my muscles are the size of Shrek's muscles, or that each muscle is individually the size of a Shrek? You're not pronouncing your apostrophes properly.'

Callie scoffed, 'Oh, please, Marcus. There is only one Shrek, he has multiple muscles, the apostrophe is in the normal place.' Then she paused, unable to resist the urge to banter with him, despite the seriousness of their situation. 'And don't act like you weren't enjoying every minute of my chaos. I saw the way you handled those werewolves,' she teased, a playful smirk playing at the corners of her lips.

He arched a masculine eyebrow, a smirk of his own tugging at his firm yet sensual mouth as he closed the distance between them. 'Admiring my muscles, were you?' he quipped, his eyes sparkling with mischief as he stepped into her personal space, the heat of his proximity sending a wave of electricity coursing through her.

She met his gaze head-on, her heart pounding in her chest as she resisted the urge to reach out and touch his pecs. 'Don't flatter yourself, Marcus. I couldn't miss your muscles if I were looking from a mile away,' she shot back, her voice laced with half-ironic sensual mischief as she tried to mask the raw attraction simmering beneath the surface.

As she met his gaze with a mixture of defiance and longing, she knew that no matter how hard she tried to fight it, Marcus had ignited a fire within her that she couldn't extinguish. In those glittering eyes, she could see that he could see that she knew.

He stepped up against her, the heat radiating off him as his breath fanned over her face, smelling of mint and leather. 'But you're not a mile away, are you, Callie? And I'm not an ogre . . .' Undeniable chemistry crackled between them, drawing them together like magnets.

Callie took a breath. 'No,' she murmured, 'you're a werewolf bodyguard with a chip on his shoulder and a hard-on for monogamy, and I'm a stone-cold bitch with no fixed address, who's not looking for anything serious.' Marcus growled. For someone who claims to be a stone cold bitch you sure smell like you're hot for something.

He kissed her.

And in that moment, as they stood locked in a battle of wills and mouths, Callie realised that no amount of sass could extinguish the blazing inferno of their desire.

Oh shit.

A Passion for Passion

GET YOUR BITS IN
[American, Modern]

Get Your Bits In *is a riotous romp through the world of modern America with a classically rugged hero and sassy plus-sized heroine combo updated for today's high-tech world.*

Salandra is a humble Etsy merchant with a lust for e-commerce and a lushly curved figure. She spends her days working on her laptop in a local coffee shop, jacked up on caffeine and hope. She fantasises quietly about the other customers in the coffee shop but she knows at the ripe old age of twenty-four, her time for youthful romance has passed. Little does she know that her café crush, looming romantically over his laptop on the next table over, is Hank.

Hank is a half-vampire, half-tech billionaire keeping his feet on the ground by working from a café whose IP he owns. When Hank's business rivals from the supernatural underground stage a violent takeover of the coffee shop, Salandra is drawn into an age-old conflict by Hank's side.

Can she overcome her small-town Etsy prejudices against tech billionaires to listen to her heart?

Can Hank overcome his rigid schedule of intermittent fasting, high-intensity interval training and paleo-blood orgies and let love in even though it might mean an unoptimised life?

Thrill as they initially resist and then ultimately succumb to the passion that flares between them.

Laugh at the hilarious misunderstanding where he

America [Modern]

tormentedly confesses that he's a vampire and she thinks he's just admitting to the role that Silicon Valley entrepreneurs play in propagating late-stage consumer capitalism while purporting to disrupt it.

Puzzle **as the vampire conglomerate tries to launch a search engine.**

Get Your Bits In, a modern Romance, is on sale now in online newsagents and children's toy megastores.

A Passion for Passion

BALLS IN THE AIR
[American, Sport]

Balls in the Air *is a modern Contemporary Romance with a sports team drama.*

Joe's a Big Leagues player in the Chicago Animals. He's got the best arm in the business and the best butt too. But his public persona as a care-for-nothing playboy is a well-manicured illusion, hiding beneath it a man who just wants to be the best he can be. They've just won the finals, so why does he feel so empty inside?

Sienna is a local Chicago nursing student, working as a bar girl to make ends meet. She's just found out her fiancé is cheating on her and is out for a rebound fling.

When Joe rescues Sienna from a sexually aggressive umpire on his team's night out, they fall into each other's arms for what each of them thinks is a no-strings-attached fling. But somehow the meaningless sex is the most meaningful sex either of them has ever had, and they are both shaken to discover that the next day they want to spend the day together going to art galleries and having breakfast in each other's t-shirts. Strings very much attached!

Soon, Joe must find a date to the awards ceremony and Sienna needs a revenge boyfriend for her cousin's upcoming wedding, and they agree to pretend to be going out in a way that would be totally acceptable to everyone including themselves if it were real. But it isn't. But is it?! Could it be?

Find out in *Balls in the Air*. Available now in all catcher's mitts.

America [Modern]

FERTILISED IN THE BILLIONAIRE'S GARDEN
[Horticulture, Frenemies-to-Lovers]

Fertilised in the Billionaire's Garden *is second in the 'Sexed-Up Dirty Fingers Clean Hearts' series of Horticultural Romances with a supernatural twist.*

Champion competitive show gardener Helliot Vrang swore she'd never get back in the hothouse after one tragic night. But then the guy she hates but can't stop thinking about accepts a gardening duel to the death in her honour.

Suddenly Helliot has to train Foxton Edge, the billionaire boy next door with a killer smile and abs for miles who broke her heart so many years ago.

Foxton is keeping a dark secret from Helliot – the story that his great-uncle ran off with her grandmother, who was the gardener on his family's estate, and that ever since then the grounds have been cursed to alkaline soil, but winning best garden in her name is his shot at breaking the curse. Will gardening bring these two ex-lovers-cum-rivals together to turn them into ex-rival-cum-lovers and break the family curse? Who'll take whom to flowerbed?

A Passion for Passion

THE SORCEROR NEXT DOOR OF MY DREAMS

[Slow Burn, Passionate Stalking, Modern]

Feisty flame-haired virgin HR manager Rowina has a new, hot neighbour who seems too good to be true: a man who makes her feel extremely physically aroused every time she sees him, who appears in her sexy dreams and who seems to spend a lot of time staring at her hotly through the curtains at night. Not in a creepy way, in a sexy, emotionally available way, which we can tell by the fact that she finds it hot rather than intrusive.

But DeForest Tycheon is even more than he seems. A half-sorceror, half-leprechaun detective, he's a sort of man with a very plan. First he has to find the evil renegade wizard Lancho he's tracked to Fayetteville, Arkansas, of Suburban America, and second, he needs to claim the woman next door as his own.

He can feel in his sorcerous leprechaun blood that she is fated to be his sexpot of gold. Until the wizard Lancho turns the tables, the hunter becomes the hunted, and suddenly Rowina is in danger of more than just the saucy dreams that spill over nightly from her sensual neighbour's leprechaun telepathy. She begins to see visions of a terrible future, affecting her performance at work, but who can she turn to? Who HRs the HR themselves?

Now DeForest knows that he cannot wait any longer. **To claim the woman his heart and soul burn for, he has**

America [Modern]

to tell her who he is, what he wants, what he is and that she has to bang him if she wants to live.*

Rowina will have to accept him with no idea of what his Myers-Briggs personality type is, and without a proper interview process! Her life – and her HR career – depends on it.

'*The Sorceror Next Door of My Dreams* is a must-not-miss'†
– *Guardian*‡

---

* His protective aura can only be transmitted through passionate banging.

† 'Must-Not-Miss' was one of my high-school nicknames. But in this instance the blurb quote is slightly misleading, as it was part of a *Guardian* gonzo battle testing feature on the most accurate books in ballistic warfare. The aerodynamic, trebuchet-friendly shape of *The Vampire Next Door of My Dreams*, as well as its heft and slick cover art, meant that it accurately out-hit such classics as *Ulysses*, *The Complete Works of Shakespeare* and Michael Crichton's *Dinosaur Park*.

‡ D'Ancey's book covers often include write-ups from papers of note, but it's important to remember D'Ancey is operating in another dimension. In this instance, the *Guardian* indicates a worldwide news publication called the *Guardian of Humanity Against the Eight*, targeted at an audience of readers united mainly in their anti-Octopus-Person sentiment and a species essentialism that would turn out either to be deeply xenophobic or genuinely prophetic. The culture section of the *Guardian* in D'Ancey's universe therefore tends to be somewhat haphazard and heavily populated with recipes for calamari dishes, which could be considered an act of provocation amounting to a declaration of war, had the Octopus People read it. Fortunately for humanity (at least for a while), the presence of ink on a page tended to have a triggering effect on Octopus-Person ink glands, causing them to respond to the perceived threat by squirting the paper they were presented with in ink of their own. This caused problems for the signing of treaties but protected humanity from its own publications.

A Passion for Passion

The Sorceror Next Door of My Dreams is already getting rave reviews, so be sure to make it part of your shameful Kindle reading on your next commute. It's available only online, to be downloaded in all good newsagents and bad bookshops.[*]

---

[*] An extraordinary feat of geolocation and geolocking, the technology required to fulfil the publication contract for this text led to programmes now used by secret services around the world to track and trace suspects, as well as preventing those suspects from downloading movies and games within 500 m of any pie shop.

What Is America?

America is a made-up place, even for Americans. The America in books is a fantasy land, full of romance and possibility. America is a lovely dreamscape full of tropes and locations and character types that have never been real and never will be real. That said, America tells its own stories so much that we know an American when we see one.

The America of Romance novels is full of honourable SEALs and six-foot-four returning soldiers whose PTSD can be cured by the love of a good woman. The America of Romance novels is full of 1950s rural charm and charming city-slicking mobsters with hearts of gold.*

The America of Romance novels can be in fast-talking

---

* They never tell you what they slick the city *with*. In the America of Romance novels, hearts of gold are a dime a dozen, which might explain inflation, if there were such a thing in the America of Romance novels, which there isn't.

A Passion for Passion

New York in black and white, where sassy enemies become sassy lovers, or in sepia tones, where a slow-talking shy cowboy holds his hat in his hands as he asks a lady to the hoedown, or in full technicolour with a dance number, or with a full perm and some Vaseline on the lens and a floaty gown while dealing with a divorce.

The America of Romance novels is peopled by people who live in the city but never weep about rent or who live in the suburbs but never worry about health insurance or the social impact of prescription OxyContin.

In the America of Romance novels, people wear chunky-knit sweaters that never itch, and drive in big cars. America is very sexy, and the food is home-made, even in diners where the worn-down waitresses take pride in their work and bring you hot strong coffee when you're having a crisis. It sounds like a great place to fall in love. The dreamy Americans in the dream America give us all hope for a world where that America could exist.

America

[Historical]

THE FEMME FALCON
[American, Noir, Feminism]

Thirty-fourth in LaGuarde's groundbreaking series of feminist detective Historical Romance Noir Thrillers with a supernatural twist, 'Dames Up to Here', The Femme Falcon *is set in the 'black-and-white' period of American history and follows the story of Hildeblanc, a gritty female detective dame with legs up to her hips and a taste for violent vigilantism.*

Hildeblanc is a hard-bitten ex-cop's ex-wife, detectiving the mean streets of supernatural Chicago to make ends meet. She has a lust for justice and a mean right hook. She spends her nights fighting crime and her days sassily smoking cigarettes while sensually fondling her extremely phallic gun and waiting for crime o'clock. She's getting by until Gramian walks into her life.

A Passion for Passion

Gramian: a doe-eyed Sam with lips up to here and a face to match, he has a mysterious past, a wizard mob family, an ancient spell book, sixteen dollars in coins, and amnesia.

They immediately have extremely consensual feminist sex and then Gramian cries manly-ly while Hildeblanc holds him and fondles her gun.

Hildeblanc must help Gramian to reclaim his memories and his rightful place as a mafia wizard prince while they explore their passionate connection all over the desk. Until they find out that Gramian is betrothed to be married into a different mafia wizard gang to broker a mafia peace. This is way above Hildeblanc's pay grade but she demands and gets a pay raise so the plot can continue.

When Gramian is kidnapped by his betrothed's hench-thugs, Hildeblanc must dive into the dark side of her feminine power (which is just to the left of the g-spot) to rescue the man she's rapidly realising she loves, but in an empowering way. A moving feminist masterpiece with a heartbreaking cameo from Hildeblanc's godmother, the revenant ghost of Mary Wollstonecraft.

The Femme Falcon is available in all feminist bookstores and tampon-dispensing machines in women's public toilets.

America [Historical]

A COWBOY CALLED HOME
[America, Second-Chance Romance, Rural]

The third in D'Ancey's 'Blood, Sex and Cattle' series of prairie Romances, it is set in the Anne of Green Gables/rancher period of history during America's golden age that never existed.

A Cowboy Called Home is the passionate tale of two hearts, one home and 1,300 head of cattle. Tex is an embittered cowboy returning to his family ranch only to find it already occupied by the last woman he wants to see. The woman who broke his heart.

Delilah has been living on Paradise Ranch for five years, her retreat from the world that betrayed her when her sister was kidnapped by a moustachioed villain and last seen tied to a set of train tracks outside Little Town, Oklahoma.

Delilah used her trust-fund money to buy Paradise Ranch because it was the site of her youthful summer romance with the son of a handsome Black rancher. Although she was forced to cut short her burgeoning teen romance by her strict and racist father, breaking both her heart and his, she remembers Paradise fondly, though she remains haunted by the loss of her sister, as well as the legendary Paradise ghost. When Tex appears she immediately offers him a job even though she wants to offer him her heart.

After her brutal teen rejection of him, Tex assumes Delilah couldn't ever love him even though she is constantly watching him bathe in the pond and demanding that he hold her at night after ghost incidents. Tex and Delilah must work

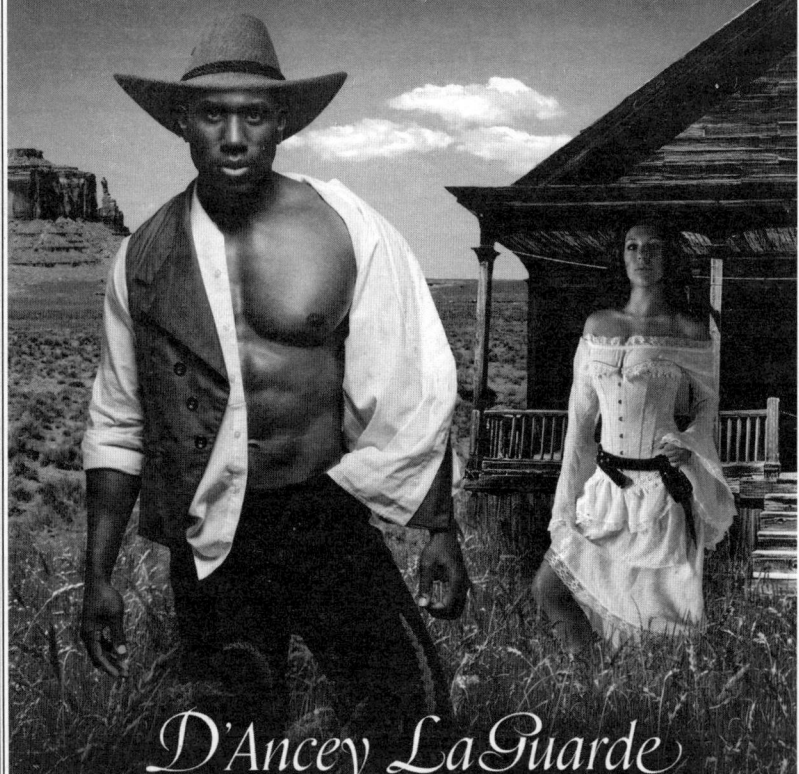

America [Historical]

sweat-inducingly closely despite their troubled past and the tensions caused by the moderately racist locals.

Together they must muster the cattle, lay to rest the ghosts of the ranch, save Delilah's miraculously still-alive but villainously traumatised sister, who was the one pretending to be the ghost, and soften the hearts of the racist townsfolk, who assume they're having sex even though they're not having sex until one day they have an emotionally honest conversation during an extremely complex cattle-birthing scene and they make passionate, post-calving field love. They succumb to their redeemed longing in some long grass. You would think this would resolve the narrative but that's only the first six chapters.

D'Ancey's epic Romance of non-specific American history is a page-turning thrill ride of lust, longing and cattle-herding logistics that will change your mind about something, probably. Read it to find out what.

The Times called *A Cowboy Called Home* 'deeply historically ambiguous'.

The *Guardian* said, 'We're not sure if cows can do that.'

A Cowboy Called Home is available now in all feedlots and hay bales.

Novelty

There are some D'Ancey books that have made it into our dimension but are impossible to categorise. Experimental books, in form, or genre-breaking books. Romance can be a very restrictive form, and D'Ancey has been at the forefront of exploring new creative territory, whether it's a cookbook or a *Where's Wally*-style graphic novelette.* Here are some of our favourites.

---

* In America, this book franchise is known as *Where's Waldo?*, but they're wrong.

Novelty

THE LOST DUKE
[Postmodernism, Redemption]

The Lost Duke *is a graphic novelette that explores the crossover between steamy Romance and children's entertainment books.**

The duke is wearing buckskin breeches, glossy boots and a high neck cravat tied in the mathematical style, and his windswept hair is impeccably beautiful. Find him in a series of complex, era-specific pictures so that he can return to his ancestral estates and save the tormented Lady Cassandra from her day job as an impoverished relation bringing knitting to her merciless cousin Lady Frumplesby.†

Pursue the duke through a series of ballrooms, gambling dens, gentlemen's clubs and horse races so he can look past

---

*   Genre crossovers like *The Lost Duke* and *Once a Pond-er Time* cemented D'Ancey as a giant of postmodernism among literary scholars. The scandalousness of elevating (or degrading) traditionally child-like mediums was seen as truly revolutionary, and led to the first mixed-media D'Ancey exhibit at the Tate Modern, which then unfortunately burned down due to an excess of sexiness.

†   The scheming Lady Frumplesby is one of the few D'Ancey villains NOT to be redeemed through the rehabilitative banging of a good (and sexy) love interest in a secondary spin-off text. Perhaps LaGuarde was just too successful in creating a truly unlikeable character, with neither intriguing eyes nor a suitably exculpatory traumatic backstory. Perhaps, on the attempt, Lady Frumplesby approached the author in the ether with the characteristic catch-cry of, 'Oh *do* fuck off, you disgusting scum,' with which she frequently dismissed the serving staff.

Lady Cassandra's apparent lack of status to the super-hot noblewoman within.

Where is he in this complicated picture? Is he top left-hand corner behind that stylish barouche? No, that's his rival, the charming but roguish Viscount Slatterly. Can't you see that coat of arms, duh!

Is he at the bottom left, tupping that wench in a house of ill repute? Of course not! That's Lady Cassandra's wastrel brother Hugo, the very reason she's been forced below her station into the demeaning but acceptably genteel position of Lady's Companion. Better get your shit together, Hugo, before Cassandra is forced to accept Viscount Slatterly's cynical offer of a loveless marriage.

Is that the duke?

Buy D'Ancey LaGuarde's *The Lost Duke* and find out. Available in all children's and adult bookstores.

Novelty

WE MADE IT ONE NIGHT
[Cookbook, Erotica]

Known for expanding the traditional forms of the Romance novel genre, We Made It One Night *is a new LaGuarde excursion that blurs the line between adult imaginative erotica and cookbooks. Part-fiction, part-cookery instruction manual, part-witch's grimoire, it puts the chemistry into chemistry, the sensuality into home economics, and the magic into creamy aphrodisiac cheesecake.*

Meet Nigella, a fictionalised character based on the famous home chef, whose passion for cooking hearty food to be enjoyed by her friends at casual yet lavish dinner parties is only exceeded by her passion for sex. Travel with Nigella through entrees, mains and desserts in her search for the one man who will whisk her heart away and clean the dishes of her difficult past.

As you move through vegetarian options, you'll meet Dale, a meaty viscount who lived more than 300 years ago. His passionate love letters intersperse the measurements conversion section until a postmodern palimpsest brings him into the present after a bungled meringue opens a portal between times and unites two hearts destined to be together.

Will Nigella and her creamy breasts figure out the recipe to send him back to his own time in time to avert a terrible disaster? Or can she successfully emulsify his barriers and stir him into her life? How many dishes can they sweep passionately to the floor as, overcome by lust, they bang on a batch of kneaded bread dough? Can Dale prove his love for Nigella and bring her back to his time, a time that truly appreciates a creamy breast and a lust for cast-iron cookware?

Find out in *We Made It One Night*, available now in the scraps bin of all commercial kitchens.

Novelty

THE MOB BOSS'S CAPTURED CONCUBINE[*]
[Second Person, Experimental]

The fact is, the economy is a nightmare, and the days of working your way up through the ranks of a company which is as loyal to you as you are to it seem as pleasingly romantic and feudal as the Romantic or Feudal periods. You're just out of university, with a degree in Media Studies, and your options look bleak.

You've looked for way longer than you'd ever admit at ads for life (nude) modelling because they look quite lucrative, and the only reason you haven't sent in your CV is that they've asked for a CV and, really, being rejected for life (nude) modelling on the strength of your CV would be more heartbreaking than the time your beloved grandmother told you Media Studies sounded like a made-up degree for fairies and you found out either your beloved grandmother hates the arts, or that your beloved grandmother is a homophobe, or that your beloved grandmother believes in fairies but thinks they're second-class citizens.

Your attention is caught by an ad in the paper for an

---

[*] This is a D'Ancey anomaly – the only book we've found where the entirety of the text, including the publicity material, is written in the second person. The sex scenes are also somehow simultaneously graphic and completely non-descriptive of genitalia. Scholars debate whether this was an experimental phase, a dissociative moment or simply D'Ancey once more pushing the bounds of sexiness to make the book's romance completely open to anyone of any gender identity.

executive assistant in running a black-market human fighting ring. Let's be fair, it's neither more unethical nor more dehumanising than 80 per cent of available corporate jobs right now. You call and are immediately struck by the manly reassuring sexiness of the voice on the other end of the line.

His name is Roman, and he's a six-foot-five crime lord with eyes made for sun and a mouth made for smoochin'. When he's not viciously murdering his opponents, he's looking at you like you're cream on a cat and that's something he finds sexy, presumably because he's also a metaphorical cat.[*] He makes you an offer you could refuse but don't want to.

Suddenly you're caught up in a world you never planned for, the concubine of a crime lord, all your dreams turned upside down and banged over a table. Can you sex him out of his evil ways, or will his delicious abs and sense of honour draw you into this life of betrayal, mystery and lust?

Find out now in *The Mob Boss's Captured Concubine*.

---

[*] To be clear, in this story, Roman is a man and not a cat at all. This is worth clarifying because it is, after all, a D'Ancey LaGuarde novel.

Novelty

A HILL TO CALL MY OWN
[Unspecified Scottish, Ecosexuality]

A Hill to Call My Own is the thirty-third installation in LaGuarde's groundbreaking new year's epic family saga, 'A Home Among the Hills', which follows the generations of the Hills family through troubled times, romance and supernatural thrills.

Kaitriona is the feckless freckled barefoot red-headed whimsical heir to the Hills family gift: the gift of being able to see her fated mate in a mug of soup on her eighteenth birthday. But the mate she sees in her mug looks like a barren hill, and Kaitriona decides she will never marry.

Until she meets Derazander.

Derazander is a wanted viscount with the face of a wastrel, a thin elegant moustache and a dark secret.

By day he's the toast of the town: half-warrior, half-aristocrat, all-man. By night he's the same, but during the afternoons of the week of the full moon he is closed for maintenance and turns into a moderately sized but elegantly contoured piece of parkland. Half-man, half-hill, he's the unexpected offspring of a woman cursed by her ex-lover: the earth spirit of a local hillock.

When Kaitriona, wandering barefoot onto her neighbouring estate while refusing to attend her curtsying lesson, is chased by a gang of wild dogs into a shrubbery, she finds herself fainting up the handsomest tree as the full moon rises. But she awakens in the warm arms of a stranger and her heart is lost. Derazander is drawn to the passionately unconventional bosom and earth-stained feet of Kaitriona Hills but cannot commit to anything but a few desperate smooches and some light but tender humping until he has broken his family curse.

And the local council of nasty lords has just given permission for a railroad that will run right through the groin of his ancestral lands. Can Kaitriona overcome her free spirit enough to negotiate local council bylaws to save her lover's elegant topography? Can Derazander find it in himself to be the man she needs him to be at a particularly important afternoon tea, and not the parkland his cursed blood demands?

With a sweeping cameo by the benevolent Isambard Kingdom Brunel, and a passionate dissertation on the influence of Capability Brown on English hillscape gardening, *A Hill to Call My Own* is a classic for the ages.

The Times called it 'upsettingly erotic'.

Wired called it 'more focused on irrigation than I expected'.

The *Guardian* called it 'possibly problematic, but we can't put our finger on why'.

A Hill to Call My Own is available now in all compost bins and socially distanced bookstores.

Create Your Own D'Ancey

To play this, please equip yourself with however many dice you need to have twenty possible numbers. Roll for each column, and then use the result as a suggestion to write your own D'Ancey LaGuarde tribute book (book-writing skills not provided). The winner is the person with the best book deal.

	Love Arc	They Bang Because	It's Set In	The Villain Is
1.	Friends to Lovers	A Storm or Other Thing Forces Them to Share a Bed	The Future	Debonair
2.	Enemies to Lovers	Must Bang to Live	The Future [dystopian]	Society
3.	Frenemies to Lovers	They Have a Fight and the Tension Breaks Their Iron Self-Control	The Future [post-apocalyptic]	An Effete Lordling
4.	Bodyguard to Lovers	Someone's Clothes Get Wet or Ripped	The Future [a spaceship]	A Brutish Lord
5.	Marriage of Convenience	They Must Pretend to Smooch to Distract Pursuers	The Future [galactic empire]	A Spurned Suitor
6.	Fake Relationship to Satisfy Social Expectations	Fate Requires It	The Past	A Jealous Ex-Lover
7.	Stuck Together! Trapped!	One or Both of Them Receive an Aphrodisiac Drug	The Past [unspecified Scotland]	An Evil Secret Society
8.	Forbidden Love	One of Them Loses a Bet	The Past [Regency]	Your Own Moral Code
9.	Best Friend's Brother	Will Someone Rid Me of this Troublesome Virginity?	The Past [Victorian]	The War
10.	Brother's Best Friend	An Explosion Throws One on Top of the Other	A Fantasy Realm	The Empire
11.	Noble Guard Captain/Protector to Lovers	They Are Stuck in a Cupboard	A Modern Fairy Tale Reboot [Three Little Pigs, But They're the Mafia and They're Hot]	A Vampire Council
12.	Love Triangle	Healing from an Injury	The Present But Supernatural Creatures Exist	The Werewolf Mafia

	Love Arc	They Bang Because	It's Set In	The Villain Is
13.	Love Octagon	They Must Consummate a Marriage of Convenience	An Academy	The Normal Mafia
14.	Amnesia	Their Captors Demand They Bang as Part of a Depraved Sex Show	On the Road, Alone in Nature, Away from the Troublesome Mores of Their Restrictive Society	An Inability to Communicate
15.	Sold to Hero By Profligate Relative in a Losing Game of Chance	His Inner Wolf Must Lay Claim to its Fated Mate	The Past [Mediaeval]	A Dark Secret from His/Her Past
16.	Christmas Redemption of Big-City Sociopath	He Wins the Championship	Underwater	Her Belief That She Cannot Have Children
17.	Amnesia	It's ⅓ or ⅔ of the Way Through the Book	A Circus [Victorian]	His Refusal to Have Children Because of His Belief That He Will Be a Bad Father Because His Parents Were Distant or Abusive
18.	Post-Military-PTSD-to-Lovers-Pipeline	She Doesn't Think She's Beautiful and He Can't Use Words to Prove How Beautiful She Is to Him So Uses His Penis	A Magical Boarding School or University	A Misunderstanding
19.	Reluctant Quest Partners	They Both Suddenly Accidentally Find Out They're Both Gay	An American Farm [Period Unspecified but Pre-Texting]	His Pride
20.	Royalty in Disguise to Lovers	One of Them Has a Nightmare and the Other Must Investigate	A Remote Community With Some Dark Secrets [But Not Too Many, and Fairly Easily Resolved; This IS Romance]	Her Prejudice

Short Stories

ONCE A POND-ER TIME
[*Short stories, Experimental*]

Discover the genre-busting Once a Pond-er Time, *a series of fairy tales set in or near a pond and rewritten for the modern age. D'Ancey answers all the questions left unanswered by traditional folklore with steamy sex scenes, heart-pounding action sequences, and complete rewriting of the facts, scenarios, characters and morals of the original texts you loved as a child. Let's be honest, that's probably for the best.*

What happens when a frog kisses a frog? Find out in *Once a Pond-er Time.*

Why hasn't anyone ever tried writing a forty-page homoerotic, sadomasochistic bang-fest with all the wicked stepmothers of all your favourite wicked-stepmother stories

Short Stories

at a special British girls' boarding school?* They have, and you'll see why in *Once a Pond-er Time*.†

How does a mermaid fuck?‡ Find out more than you've ever wanted to know in *Once a Pond-er Time*.

'For those who have time or pond scum on their hands, this book will reach deep into the silkily silted depths of your heart and loins, and let bloom the warm wet lilies of desire' — *The Daily*§

---

* When challenged about the age-appropriateness and consent issues of writing fiction set in a boarding school where every single character is having sex an extraordinary amount of the time, D'Ancey responded first 'it's fine', then that the characters are all timeless, ageless archetypes, and third that it's the kind of boarding school that only accepts people over the age of twenty-one. As we can't be sure which ages are schooled in D'Ancey's dimension, we just have to accept the assertion that 'it's fine'.

† You think you want to know where the pond fits into this one, but trust me, you don't. Just accept that it's there and move on with your life still able to look a duck in the eye.

‡ Unfortunately for the reader, *Once a Pond-er Time* is one of the texts that has never crossed the dimensional barrier into our own universe, so D'Ancey's particular solution to this age-old problem remains out of our reach. Regular human man Josh Gondelman has this to say about the issue: 'I feel like it would be tough to date as a mermaid because I feel like if you're dating non-mermaids, whoever you're dating will just assume you're gonna do a lot of mouth stuff.'

§ Until this time a paper of note, *The Daily* immediately collapsed as a business directly after the publication of this review due to backlash at its 'unacceptably horny' language and the accompanying explicit cartoons that had been submitted sketched in the margins of the hand-scrawled review and let through to the page by a flustered copyeditor. An unfortunate loss

A Passion for Passion

'Moist' — *The Times*

'I can never look a duck in the eye again' — *Sun*

'Unputdownable, and for all the wrong reasons' — BookTok

Once a Pond-er Time: Find it at all participating booksellers and cheap bed and breakfasts.*

---

to the journalism community, all the more so as we never found out the answer to the question, '*The Daily what?*'

* It is a difficult thing in a cost-of-living crisis to determine what constitutes a 'cheap bed and breakfast'. Apparently the distinction is something like the difference between erotica and pornography, which is to say, you know it when you see it.

Short Stories

THE GREEK BARON'S PREGNANT CONCUBINE AND OTHER SHORT STORIES
[Short stories, Problematic]

The Greek Baron's Pregnant Concubine and Other Short Stories *is a compilation of short stories set as spin-offs from LaGuarde's most popular and beloved worlds.*

Including 'The Cog and the Lady', an intriguing short story that combines espionage, romance, betrayal and illegal magic, set in a steampunk alternate czarist Russia, where Nikolai Nikolayevich, the seductive Siberian assassin, protects and then falls in love with Baby Yaga, the feisty yet vulnerable runaway princess and secret daughter of evil witch Baba Yaga.

And 'Ladies! Ladies! Ladies!', a perfect story for when you need some mediaeval-era lesbian paranormal escapism with a side of seventh-century monastic mystery.

And 'The Lost Duke's Last Loves', an aristocratic Victorian polyamorous Romance between Hadrian, Lord Apollo, a self-loathing rake who falls for a bisexual industrialist crime-lord-made-good, Indigo Wetherby, and then also falls for Indigo's ex-childhood sweetheart, now sworn enemy, disgraced courtesan Lady Delilah Preen.

In these stories and many more, there's something to tingle everybody's loins in a massively sweaty compilation of beloved D'Ancey characters.

The Place of the Penis in Romance Novels

In a word: Secondary.

The place of the penis in Romance novels is secondary; it may act as a sort of lodestone for the hero to guide him to his proper mate because he, however rakish or jaded or restrained or dutiful, will find the heroine irresistibly inflaming to it. This is traditionally because of her extreme beauty and hand-spannable waist, but in more recent years of Romance novels, it may be because of her inner beauty, his outspoken ways or their refreshingly anachronistic attitude to the deeply flawed society in which they exist.

Penises in Romance are described but not envisioned; they exist only in their emotional impact on the heroine.* The vagueness of penis-description can be attributed to a number of things:

---

* Of course, some romances occur between penisless individuals, in which case this chapter may safely be left uninserted.

The Place of the Penis in Romance Novels

1. There is no objectively correct size or shape for a penis; the reader must feel free to insert their own penis into the relevant passages for maximum comfort.
2. It is impossible to explain the penis or describe it accurately in isolation in a way that isn't either funny, menacing or evocative of a painful inflammation. For this we can blame medical science and teenage boys.
3. In Romance, the penis is occasionally metonymy, and one ought never to try to measure a metonym.

If the penis intrudes on the consciousness of the heroine before it is demanded for an act of loving consummation, it is there to be manfully restrained as an act of service until the heroine is ready to receive it.* It's refreshing in a world where penisness drives so much culture to see the organ put on the back burner, narratively speaking. Penises rarely drive the plots of Romance, emotions do. In a way, it is some part of the hero's quest in Romance to manage his own penis until it's required by the demands of the narrative. They do not require maintenance or supervision or apology. They are noble, sometimes proud, but always reliable. They fail only when a hero is trying to bury his sorrows in the wrong person.

---

* If a hero penis ever causes discomfort, the reader can be assured it will return soon after and function as the tool whereby the discomfort is repaired.

A Passion for Passion

QUIZ YOUR FAMILY

Q: *Are the following descriptions of penises in Romance novels?*

1. 'Steel wrapped in Silk'
2. '... stood up as a proud member'
3. '... surged forward to find its home'
4. 'Towering Manhood'
5. '... two swan's eggs in a black nest'

Answers

1. Historical description of a new kind of corset; 1890s fashion magazine *La Mode Illustrée*
2. Hansard 1820, remarks made by the Member of Parliament for Crawley
3. 1790s description of HMS *Beneficence,* upon its triumphant launch
4. Surprisingly, HMS *Towering Manhood* was also a sailing vessel, though it was lost in a mermaid incident in the 1830s
5. Genuine description of testicles in a Romance novel

Sci-Fi / Future

THEY CAME FROM ABOVE
[Sci-Fi, Fated Mates, Galactic]

Eleventh in D'Ancey LaGuarde's 'Guys From the Sky' Science-Fiction Romance Thriller alien soul-bond series, They Came From Above *is a groundbreaking space-thumping hump-fest set 60 million kilometres from home.*

Bevlon is a reckless alien navigator from the fascistic warrior planet Glaybius 5, on the run from a ruthless galactic government. Fifty years ago he exposed a secret Glaybian plot to betray their own galactic troops and has been on the run ever since. He roams the universe selling his sword and then buying it back again with money he gets from other jobs and from seducing powerful women for their secrets. When he crash-lands on Terra 3, an Earth colony, he meets Max, an innocent farmstress, uneducated in the ways of the seductive alien race.

A Passion for Passion

Max isn't even sure she believes in sexy alien warriors but this one has just landed on her porch.

Bevlon offers to pay for his bed and board with his sword but she needs a farmhand, and while she might fantasise about this particular farmhand's firm hand, she gets a firm grip on herself and they work together in bucolic harmony, slowly growing closer until she has to admit the fact that this mysterious alien reminds her of a dream she's been dreaming all her life about the sexy alien warrior who saved her father from a government plot back in the 4060s.

Bevlon has the answers she craves and says he can help her find the lost treasure of her family. Together they enter the seedy world of intergalactic slave auctions, battle a powerful alien queen whose diseased blood turns humans into cannibals, and discover a passion unlike any other. Theirs.

That's *They Came From Above*, available in every good bookshop.

Sci-Fi / Future

STAR CROWN
[Sci-Fi, Noir, Mediaeval Futurism]

Star Crown *is a futuristic Sci-Fi Noir Mystery Romance with a mediaeval twist.*

In the distant future, humanity has colonised the stars. Civilisations vastly different from one another roam the galaxy competing for resources.

Gartheon is a chalice knight, sworn to fight for justice in the darkness between systems. Equipped only with his high-tech-exoskeleton, his sentient talking laser Swiss army sword and an ancient faith in the laws of justice, he's a lone wolf and happy to stay that way. While hunting Mikreos, a rogue necromancer, through an inhabited system, his bioship is badly wounded and he must crash-land on Chaucerion.

Rindell is a bookish novice warrior nun who longs for adventure. Trapped by her culture's obsession with recreating humanity's mediaeval past, she longs for a white knight to come save her.

But when a spaceship crashes in a millpond on the estate of the nunnery, it turns out that she's the one to have to save the white knight. Finding him unconscious in the wreckage, she is drawn to his soft mouth and sensitive abs.

With both arms broken and his tech-exoskeleton missing its energy core, Gartheon has no option but to take the help of this small powerful woman to clean his groin injury and to navigate this alien world.

They bond over a love of mediaeval literature while she

puts hot poultices on his quivering crotch. But when the evil Mikreos arrives at the nunnery disguised as a seer emissary from the wizard pope and chooses Rindell as part of the queen's sacrificial virgin gladiator nun cadre, Gartheon must solve the mystery of Rindell's royal past, extract the energy source for his tech-exoskeleton from a band of evil monks and sexily train the woman he is secretly coming to love in hand-to-hand gladiatorial combat, while resisting the powerful urge to smooch her with tongue.

Will they be able to overcome their deep mutual repression to consummate their passion? What about when they realise that in order to save Rindell from death in the coliseum they must relieve her of her virginity? Mystery, history, magic, fantasy and passion collide, with a graphic sex scene in a careening chariot mid-combat, and a cameo from Rindell's godfather, an AI of Isambard Kingdom Brunel, who was the advisor to her father, who turns out to have been the previously wrongly deposed King . . . OF THE GALAXY.

Available now in the vast emptiness between the stars.

Sci-Fi / Future

SON OF THE KING OF THE GLOOM
[Postapocalyptic, America]

Son of the King of the Gloom *is number eight in D'Ancey LaGuarde's most modern supernatural Romance Thriller series.**

He's the son of an immortal warrior, she's a sassy gang leader in post-apocalyptic New New New York with a secret passion for oil painting.

Garshian is the bastard son of an immortal warrior trying to find his way in the hostile world of a post-apocalyptic New York. Heir to the heir of the Kingdom of Night, Garshian has only just found his father and is coming to terms with his new responsibilities as a half-prince, half-immortal, all-hunk when he finds Laralandra.

Laralandra is all legs and no regrets, the leather-clad leader of a violent gang of sassy vixens known as the Valkyries.

They meet one night in the middle of a criminal chase when Garshian tries to save Laralandra's spunky adopted kid sister and is wounded on one of his corners by a spear.

He then has a spear-induced vision of the future and collapses in front of a pack of ravening Brooklyn werewolves. Laralandra saves his life in gratitude for him saving the life of her spunky adopted kid sister but she's not happy about it.

---

* It is unclear whether this title is a sequel to *The King of the Gloom*, because nothing in it seems related.

A Passion for Passion

Garshian must break it to Laralandra that they are destined for a future together and that in order to save New New New York, he must awaken her immortal blood in the only way he knows how — with his penis. Laralandra refuses him and they must develop an uneasy respect for each other as they track down the gang that's trying to destroy New New New York and find out why Laralandra doesn't want a life-long bang-bond with a sexy stranger for life. But they can't fight the overpowering magnetism that draws them together and they embrace at last in a destructively intense sex scene. But before they can have their happily ever after, Laralandra must wrestle with the fact that she's eternally bonded to a sexy near-stranger while saving her sassy gang of spunky girls from the post-apocalyptic apocalypse that looms before them. Garshian in turn must learn and grow into respecting Laralandra's individuality as a post-post-modern empowered woman, oil painter and gang leader.

Sci-Fi / Future

THE FORGETFUL PRINCE'S HEROIC SEAMSTRESS
[Future, Covid, Goblins]

... *is a modern coronavirus Romance, set in a world much like our own, but where the coronavirus threat is compounded by the menace of a goblin army massing on the shores of a steampunk Chicago.*[*]

When Dalseth, the Crown Prince of Chicago, is caught away from his palace at the beginning of a lockdown, injured by goblins, he is forced to take shelter with an outcast seamstress and her adorable half-goblin child. His memory gone, he finds himself nursed back to health by the last person he would ever expect to be beholden to, but as his memory returns, he must fight against his urge to have sex with her and his inexplicable surges of wanting to murder her extremely cute and charming goblin child.

Gerania is an ex-renegade eking a modest living by making pop-culture plushies for Etsy. Outcast for the sin of loving a goblin in wartime, the simple seamstress nonetheless finds it in her heart to welcome a ragged warrior into her plucky family. But as lockdown wears on and his memory slowly returns, the love and trust building between them turns to hate, and then back to love, and then to sex, and then back to hate, and then back to Happily Ever After.

---

[*]   A remarkably PG-rated novel from D'Ancey LaGuarde. Not as . . . sweaty as they usually are, academics speculate that this was an attempt at YA fiction.

Time Travel

THE QUARTZEN QUEENDOM
[Time Travel, Sexy Nuns, Sapphic]

Sixteenth in D'Ancey LaGuarde's 'Twinkle Twinkle Laser Fire Time Warp' set of time-travelling space adventure Romance Thriller novels, The Quartzen Queendom *is set in the far future.*

High priestess Beglinker was raised on a convent planet to be the Chosen One, the only human with the ability to communicate with black holes, but when a fleet of monstrous hive-mind lizards from the evil empire known only as the Bleak destroys her planet, she is fired off into space in a capsule, the sole survivor of her peaceful race of sexy nuns.

One thousand years later, space mercenary Harjohn Flindersman finds Beglinker capsule floating in the vastness of the Forbidden Zone and rescues her in the hope of a reward. While hardened femme warrior Harjohn's lack of deference due to a sexy nun/Chosen One at first affronts

Time Travel

the corseted Beglinker, she is reluctantly impressed by the ancient nun's surprising competence at basically everything, her sassy mouth and her ability to communicate with black holes. Harjohn's cynical approach to the world hides her vulnerability, in a way that is similar to but definitely not infringing on the copyright of Han Solo. She agrees to help Beglinker in her quest for knowledge and vengeance, and their mutual distrust turns to mutual lust. When the Bleak arrests Harjohn for being a charming ruffian, Beglinker must rescue her in turn, but in the heat of the battle, in fear for the life of the ruffianly woman she suddenly realises she has fallen for, she, temporarily summons a black hole that threatens to eat the universe. As a sexy nun, her ravening uncontrolled power can only be stopped by Harjohn's love and she delivers control over her power along with her virginity into the spacewoman's seductive hands. But the proximity to the black hole has cast them into a different time and place. Together they begin a long trek home in a way that is similar to but definitely not infringing on the copyright of *Star Trek Voyager*.

Join Beglinker and Harjohn on their continuing adventures through the Forbidden Zone of Love.

A Passion for Passion

OUT OF TIME AND IN HIS ARMS
[Time Travel]

Out of Time and in His Arms *is the fifth of the twenty-four-book 'Time Travellers' Mistresses' series. An Ahistorical Romance with a supernatural twist,* Out of Time and in His Arms *is a swashbuckling frenemies-to-lovers romp through a sexy steampunk universe full of excitement, boners and rogue dinosaurs.*

Dr Rafe Semantic is a young professor of time travel, recently recruited into the Academy of Time's Secret Institute's Time Spies League of Improbably Hot Brothers in Arms.* Passionately devoted to saving the world from chrono-terrorists, he has all the time in the world to fight, but none for love. **His bantering teasing of the Secret Institute's meek librarian hides a longing for the quieter, more academic life prohibited by his extreme skills and abs.**

Diantra is an eccentric but devastatingly beautiful half-librarian, half-time wizard working part time at the Academy of Time, until a chrono-terrorist kidnaps her for her encyclopaedic knowledge of encyclopaedias and her time-wizard powers.

Rescued by Rafe, their time vessel damaged by laser gunfire, they are cast adrift together on the seas of chronology with no option but to use Diantra's innate ability to navigate the

---

* You thought this was a setup for a pleasing acronym, but time spies are too cool for acronyms. It turns out being able to move through time makes linear order seem irrelevant.

time-tides only while in states of heightened passion. They are forced to bang it out constantly and professionally while trying not to fall in love. As they resolve their emotional issues by having philosophical discussions during sex scenes, they must solve the mystery of the missing pyramid, get a pivotal pterodactyl back to the late Triassic period and capture the sinister head of the chrono-anarchists, whose dangerous obsession with Diantra's bloodline threatens the very fabric of time.

With a small but relevant cameo from Isambard Kingdom Brunel, *Out of Time and in His Arms* is the feel-good hit of this . . . *and last* summer!

When you have a sexy librarian, you know it's only a matter of time before her glasses, and the wheels, and her pants come off.

Find your copy just in the corner of your eye, or in all deconsecrated bookshops.

EXTRACT FROM *OUT OF TIME AND IN HIS ARMS*

Diantra's lip quivered. 'Rafe, I have an exhaustive list of the history, archaeological discovery protocol, genus and species of the pterodactyl. I just never expected a baby one to be so cute! I will call him Terry.'

'No! Don't name him! It could interfere with the space-time prime directive!' But as Diantra was already holding the small razor-beaked dino-chick nestled in

Time Travel

the warm cavity between her creamy bosoms, Rafe spoke with resignation rather than true vigour. *Never stand between a woman and something fluffy*, he thought, slightly sexistly, but in this case annoyingly accurately. Also he wasn't entirely sure if the prime directive was a real rule or just something the Academy of Time's Secret Institute's Time Spies League of Improbably Hot Brothers in Arms had picked up from *Star Trek* and started to say to each other after one too many loose nights out gifting their seed to various assorted vestal virgins in ancient Rome.

Had Diantra been privy to his thoughts she might not have beamed at him quite so widely, nor tucked her free hand so confidingly into his larger masculine one. He looked down into the luminous pools of her eyes, shining with the acquisitive joy of both an academic satisfying her curiosity about a baby pterodactyl and a girl-who-likes-cute-things satisfying the human urge to nuzzle a baby pterodactyl. He found his neck bending, firm manly mouth drawn irresistibly downward toward her billowing softness. Had the pterodactyl baby not chosen that moment to violently evacuate its stomach contents from both ends, who knows what foolishness Dr Rafe might have found himself engaged in.

He straightened, suddenly noticing a glint from the corner of his eye! Laser gun! He leaped forward. Seizing Diantra by her tiny waist in one arm and Terry by his whole tiny head, Rafe leaped towards the door of the time machine. 'Diantra, get nude! We've gotta get out of now!'

A Passion for Passion

THE MANNERLY MATCH
[Time Travel, Historical, Forbidden Love]

The Mannerly Match *is the fifteenth in LaGuarde's 'Upskirts of History' time-travelling Romance series with a supernatural twist. Set in the Regency period of England,* The Mannerly Match *will set light to your loins with its sexy sex scenes and romantic sex scenes.*

Grace is the lord of manners *and* of the manor. An impeccably polite duke with a dark past, he's the catch of the marriage mart but is ever elusive against the scheming mammas of the haut ton who fling their frippery daughters at his slippery head in the worst game of dodgeball ever.

You can only politely replace the lunging bosom of a desperate debutante back in its corset so many times before you're caught in the web of matrimony, and Grace decides at last to wed. But whom? He retreats to his country manor to decide, but when he's held up by a gang of highwaymen, he can't help but be intrigued by the lady highwayman who roughs him up. Her small, strong, delicate, deft yet uncalloused hands bespeak a life among the aristocracy but she's got a filthy, filthy mouth and Grace thrills to her masterful mystery.*

Agnes is a woman out of time. She was a graphic designer living in Kent until she began to research her family history, and upon reading an illustrated almanack, she was flung into the past by a Glitch in the Space-Time Continuum™. F-ck.

---

* Ought this be mistressful mystery? xx D'Ancey

Time Travel

Falling in with a band of ruffians, she's making her way with highwaymannery, forever seeking a man whose sexy face she saw in her history book, and also his bottom. When she holds him up on the road, she realises that he is the man who is fated to be her eternal love and also her great-great-great-great-great-great-great-great-great-grandfather.

After a soothing handjob on horseback, he knows he ought to go on his gentlemanly way and leave her, but he's drawn to connect more meaningfully with her in an extremely anachronistic and respectful manner. Can she bear to become her own great-great-great-great-great-great-great-great-great-grandmother? Or will she discover that she has an identical cousin (no relation) who is actually her ancestor and it's all OK in the end?

A Passion for Passion

THE LOST POST
[Time Travel, Interdimensional, Future]

The Lost Post *is the 366th instalment of the 'Time Lovers' series of Alternate Historical Romance novels with a super temporal twist.*

Alice is a successful but lonely career woman podcasting news satire from a luxury space-station studio orbiting the Earth to avoid construction noise interfering with her sound quality. She's got everything a woman in a self-contained pod drifting through the endless emptiness of the void could want: job satisfaction, a sauna and a pretty solid Wi-Fi connection. Really, what more could a podcaster ask for, except a love that transcends time and space, which, with her gruelling daily schedule, she thinks would be too much. Besides, she's alone in a space station, apart from the occasional passing sauna repairman. But love is the most outer-space thing there is.

It is Lord Glitchington, the Glitch in the Space-Time Continuum™, a recently created temporal anomaly with literally everything within its grasp, but all it seems to want to do is meet a lonely and attractive space-based podcaster and carry her words across dimensional barriers and time.

At first she's suspicious of its motives, and disturbed by the quantum physics of the situation. She is haunted by a quantum childhood trauma (her childhood cat was used in a Schrödinger's box experiment and rendered both dead and alive, it roamed the Earth as a zombie cat), and she fears entrusting her heart to something that both is and is not, and Lord Glitchington must restrain its passion while simultaneously being aware of the heated potential of quantum fingering.*

Together they travel the universe, fuelled by friendship and the quantum power of will-they-won't-they-ness to right wrongs, solve mysteries and kill Adult Hitler.

She must learn to trust the quantum heart of the glitch and understand that she is and always has been the fated mate of this cosmic comedy. Travel with our star-crossing lovers together to the first time they met, and watch time, space, podcasting and destiny rub up against each other across the multiverse, sparking a thousand new worlds of imagination.

As she untangles the fractal genitalia of the glitch, it discovers workers' rights and human emotion, with hilarious results. Two completely different states of matter and quantum flux must be able to get past their differences and make creamy love across a thousand layered Milky Ways despite the parental disapproval of physics, reason and human anatomy.

With a heartbreaking cameo from the ghost of celebrity Victorian bridge-builder Isambard Kingdom Brunel.

The Lost Post is available then, now and in the future, in all good lost-luggage lockers.

---

* Is an orgasm a wave or a particle?

LGBTQ+

It has taken many years for Romance to embrace broader categories than those traditionally offered by the classic heteronormative model. Those whose loves and lusts have fallen outside of the mainest mainstream culture have in the past been forced into small printing presses, or else forced to laboriously work through Trad Romances changing every instance of gender in *The Greek Billionaire's Secret Baby* to the opposite one, by hand. Now, a thousand blossoms bloom, a wider range of people are finding their way into the sweaty imaginings of the Romance readership and every three months a person is torn to pieces by a crocodile in far North Queensland.* Part of the explosion of LGBTQ+ offerings in the Romance space can be attributed to the popularity

---

* This is a reference to Conservative Australian politician Bob Katter being forced by the tides of progress away from public bigotry, and not a reference to the other politician, Mao Zedong, who said 'Let a hundred flowers blossom' and also didn't mean it.

LGBTQ+

of Slash fan fiction online, and partly due to the increasing awareness in society that people of all genders, nationalities and orientations also want to read improbable tales of overheated passion. These people, seemingly to the surprise of book publishers, have bank accounts and will buy a range of stories.*

---

* Moreover, it turns out, bored housewives in the suburbs aren't going to shy away from a wider demographic range of abs.

A Passion for Passion

THE LORD AND HIS MAN
[Historical, Homoerotic]

The Lord and His Man *is the forty-third in LaGuarde's 'Manly Men and the Men Who Love Them' series of historical homoerotic detective Romance Thrillers with a supernatural twist.*

Lance is a lord negotiating the heterosexual pressures of the Regency marriage mart with the help of his plucky valet, Blade, a muscular man of lowly birth and mighty thews, whom Lance impulsively hired when Blade lightfingered his pocket in a back alley one stormy night. As Blade lavishes tender attention on the arrangement of his master's cravat each day, their eyes meet lingeringly but both are held back by the fear that their forbidden love is not reciprocated. Both must constantly adjust uncomfortable erections that the other consistently attributes to various buxom women in a comedy of errors and throbbing lust.

It's not until Blade's dark past returns to haunt him in the form of the helpful ghost of an ex-cat burglar ex-lover while he's helping Lord Lance bathe his creamy pecs in an anachronistically sudsy bath scene that Lance realises that he has a chance with the gentle beefcake valet who just fainted into his tub, and also . . . that Blade has magical powers. But he must solve the crimes of which Blade is accused before his heart's desire is hanged for breaking the law.

And what about Lord Pranceling, the sinister dandy who threatens to ruin Lord Lance's reputation unless he promises to spend the night at Pranceling Manor, known for its

LGBTQ+

depravities? Lord Lance has no option but to accede to sinister Pranceling's outrageous demands and slips out at night to the evil revelry, followed surreptitiously by a mighty thewed silhouette in his master's second best coat.

There, the masked perverts of the Hellfire Club menace Lance's innocence until he is swept up in the tender embrace of a mysterious man whose erection feels oddly familiar. Together, Lance and Blade must unite forces above-stairs and below to protect each other, punish Lord Pranceling and expose the Hellfire Club while also having sex.

A Passion for Passion

LORD PRANCELING'S REDEMPTION
[Gay, Redemption, Historical]

Lord Pranceling's Redemption *is the forty-fourth in LaGuarde's 'Manly Men and the Men Who Love Them' series of historical homoerotic detective Romance Thrillers with a supernatural twist.*

Lord Edgard Pranceling is a villain, a blackmailer, a dandy and a cad. His powdered wig, effete manner and ruby-encrusted heels hide a tormented soul and surprisingly ridged abdominal muscles.

His remarkable violet eyes, each framed by a separate gold quizzing glass, look sinisterly cynical, but beneath the beruffled front of his starched linens beats a wounded heart. Thwarted in his villainy by Lance and Blade in the prequel, *The Lord and His Man*, Edgard returns defeated to the Pranceling country estate to lick his pride and brood on his foiled plans and guilty regrets. There he is, riding neck-or-nothing over the menacing moors of Pranceling Manor, when he encounters an innocent country mensch in dire distress. Gullivant is a country milkman, the illegitimate child of an earl, herding his cows and suppressing his homosexual desires as well as his noble heritage.

Caught in the crossfire of a fist fight in the local inn, a head wound has left him disoriented on the moors, stricken with amnesia, and nude.

Gullivant senses he's not meant to tell anyone he's the gay heir to a vast fortune and that some element of his identity is dangerous to disclose but he can't remember which bit or why.

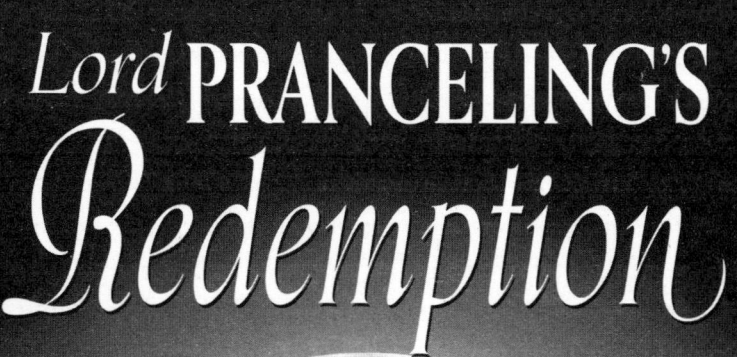

Lord **PRANCELING'S** *Redemption*

D'Ancey LaGuarde

A Passion for Passion

Lord Pranceling, infinitely villainous, sweeps up Gullivant to deprave in the cackling privacy of his own manor but is suddenly struck by tender, protective urges to shield the innocent flower of manhood who has fallen thus unwitting and unclothed into his degenerate, lace-beruffled clutches.

Pranceling's heart longs for more than just a meaningless sadomasochistic fling with an amnesiac milkman.

Gullivant, unaware of Edgard's degenerate reputation, is stricken by sexy hero worship for his noble rescuer and wishes only to succumb to the lure of his lavender eyes and abdominal array. Why then has the conscienceless Edgard suddenly been stricken by an urge to protect rather than debauch Gullivant? Could it be true love? Only by reluctantly making tender love can they possibly find out. How will Gullivant react to Pranceling's history of sinister deviance and villainous pervert cackling? Will he ever forgive the man and fall into his surprisingly muscular arms? It's not until the ghost of the family wolf emerges, let loose on the full moon from the lord's private crypt, to howl a prophecy of true love at the lowering sky that Edgard realises he may have met his mate.

With a redemptive cameo appearance from Lord Lance and his luscious valet Blade, and a heartwarming Christmas vignette with Edgard's adorably lisping adopted niece, *Lord Pranceling's Redemption* will win your heart and warm your 'nads.

LGBTQ+

STORM IN A TEACOUNT
[Bisexual Cross-Dressing]

Storm in a TeaCount *is the Victorian Romantic Thriller that will leave your panties in an inextricable, inexplicable, upsettingly damp knot.*

Escaping an unwanted arranged marriage disguised as a boy, Annelise is the wealthy daughter of a merchant, sold off to an aristocrat to improve her family's social standing in exchange for her dowry, which will repair the ruined estates of the sinister and rakish Duke of Harbouroughton. But less than three miles into her headlong cross-dressing flight from the sinister duke's estate, she stumbles upon a gentleman in the throes of being held up by a highwayman. Though she knows she should not stop, Annelise hits the highwayman with a sentimental vase she brought along on her escape before swooning in the powerful arms of the mysterious rescued nobleman. Though she fears exposure, he accepts her story without question and she is swiftly and passionately hired as a footman to the very duke she was meant to be escaping.

Hadrian is the Duke of Harbouroughton.

Thick-thighed, strong-willed and experimentally bisexual, he has carefully cultivated his reputation as a rake in order to fool the world into underestimating him while he tries to repair his family's ruined fortune through trade with the Indies, the historicosocial ethics of which we will not closely examine. But it's not until a delicate boy saves his life with an inexplicable vase that Hadrian finds his perfect match. But the boy Annetony is not of his social class, so it would be wrong to try to feel him up on a horse. Can Hadrian resist this sexy stripling, whose long-lashed eyes and effeminate mouth send sensual semaphore signals to his heart and groin?

How will Annelise reassure her family that she is safe from ruin when she is living disguised and unwed in the very halls from which she fled? Will they discover each other mid-gender bending sex and be forced to wed by her horrible family in a way they both secretly want but to which they will both strenuously object, giving the mutual false impression that they don't love each other even though they do and leading to much incredibly pointless heartache and misunderstanding?

LGBTQ+

THE OTHER WORD FOR OTTOMAN*
[Historical, Political, Homoerotic]

Third in the deeply problematic 'Ottoman Hottoman' series of Exotic Historical Homoeroticism, set in the city of Constantinople-cum-Istanbul and vice versa, The Other Word for Ottoman *is a steamy Romance set mainly in the steam rooms of a private palace of indeterminate era and vague orientalism.*

Lord Montleroy is a British diplomat, sent to be British at foreigners during political times. He is haughty, aloof and completely out of his depth amidst the sophisticated Ottoman political society he finds himself enmeshed in. That is until Suleyman, an exotic and noble exotic nobleman arrives and takes him under his embroidered wing. Lord Montleroy, while grateful to be rescued, doesn't understand that he has been placed under an obligation. A debt that can only be paid in smooches.

Suleyman is the eldest son of a noble house, escaping his family duty to wed by burying himself in the internecine politics of the Ottoman court. When Lord Montleroy crashes into his life during a disastrous banquet, Suleyman must decide whether to rescue the hapless, blue-eyed, chisel-jawed

---

* For the reader's context, this was advertised in D'Ancey's dimension as 'selling more copies than ever despite the 90 per cent reduction in the world's population, the last bastion of escapist entertainment in a world where most entertainment is just escaping from whatever horrible post-apocalyptic gang wants to turn your feet into shoes now'.

A Passion for Passion

naif, or leave him to sink. When he discovers that there's more to Montleroy than just abs and gaffes, he must cast his foreign lover aside or risk losing his status at court, and his heart.

Will Lord Montleroy return to his native shores and the disappointment of the king or will Suleyman overcome his exotic mysteriousness enough to admit that he loves this pasty foreign weirdo? Find out in *The Other Word for Ottoman*.

Available now in all questionably orientalist costume shops and in the footnotes to Edward Said texts.

Polyamory / Ménage à Trois

THE ARGUMENT FOR TRIANGLES

Often dismissed as stories for people who want to eat their cake and have it too, stories with more than one love interest can fall into the unfulfilled love-triangle model (Team Edward vs Team Jacob), or the good, the better, the best model (Team Tamlin vs Team Rhysland) in which the kind author will often pair off the spurned third in a follow-up book. Alternatively, you can just let the triangle[*] exist as a stable and valid structure in itself.

Ask any maths professor or passing Pythagoras about triangles and they'll wax lyrical about the beauty of the form. Though traditional marriages are dominant in Romance literature, there is growing room for more interesting geometries of passion, and even in a happily-ever-after that involves

---

[*] Or other polyhedron.

children (the ultimate Romance sign of success, signalling as it does the possibility of a sequel series), it's always good to have someone spare hanging around to go get the milk.

Polyamory / Ménage à Trois

THE SEALS' SEXY SEAL
[Threesome, Selkie, PTSD, Small Town]

A futuristic supernatural Navy SEALs Romance Mystery with a throuple twist.

Dane and Sebastian are SEALs, not real seals but Navy SEALs. And brothers, not real brothers but the kind of brothers you are when you're both Navy SEALs. They're bonded through the camaraderie of their elite military unit, through their shared cybernetic implants and through an ancient blood-bond ritual that should have killed them along with the rest of their unit back in the war in the unspecified place that we won't name lest it make us feel weird for romanticising these dudes' life of state-sanctioned violence or ask what they actually did for work other than sit-ups to maintain their perfectly rock-hard and mysteriously oily abs.

Loose on the road after twenty years of military service, they're looking for the home they've never had, among the people they've always protected but never truly known.

Persia is a small-town operator of Heartstone, a homely roadside inn by the Maine coastline. All she wants is a normal life in her small town, and no complications. Orphaned from birth, raised in an experimental facility, she is also a seal, which is to say not a SEAL and not a full seal but a real half-seal who has to spend time regularly both in water and on land, leaving her skin discarded on the shore. Business is slow, and she likes it that way.

A Passion for Passion

When two ab-stricken men knock at her inn's door during an ice storm, little does she know that they're about to turn her life, and her vagina, upside down.

Trapped together in the inn while the storm rages outside, Dane and Sebastian find themselves drawn to the buxom Persia, both seeing each other's love and being too honourable to act on their own, because of the SEAL bro code and their repressed love for each other. While fetching cocoa in the kitchen, Persia finds herself standing too close to Dane, mainly because of his extraordinary masculine bigness filling up most of the floor space. While selecting a book from the library, she falls from a ladder and is caught by Sebastian, who happens to be shirtless for reasons that are adequately explained in the book.

Persia is torn by the reawakening of her sexual self after years of celibacy, and equally attracted to both men. Heated dreams and scenes of furtive and variously guilty near-misses and near-kisses follow on all fronts but the triangular tension rising between them can never be indulged.

Until one day, certain she's come to some harm while 'fishing' in the freezing water of the harbour, Sebastian and Dane dive into the icy depths to look for her, immediately hypotherming themselves. They are rescued by a graceful, muscular seal who suddenly becomes a nude Persia, switching her body from sexy seal to sexy lady, and realise she may not be the conservative girl next door they'd both sexistly projected her to be. They must huddle for warmth and talk about their feelings until Sebastian and Dane realise that the love they feel for each other as bros is greater than the platonic love a SEAL

Polyamory / Ménage à Trois

ought to feel for a SEAL and the love they feel together for Persia is more profound than they ever thought three seals could feel.

Can these three sort-of seals seal a pact between them for a logistically complex but mutually satisfactory throupling? Can Dane and Sebastian resolve their complex trauma from the loss of all their comrades through the sensual embrace of a good woman? Can they protect Persia from the sinister wizard/professor who wants to kidnap and study her?

Find out in *The SEALs' Sexy Seal.*

EXTRACT FROM *THE SEALS' SEXY SEAL*

Persia's sleek eyes and giant bosom looked back at Dane, as he rested both massive man-hands on her curvaceous hips. Warmth seemed to radiate out of them and into the sides of her bottom and beyond. Not since she last made out with a whale in the ocean had she felt such a wave of lust, and here at the dinner-plate-sized hands of an ex-military American, she was both on land and totally beached. He pressed close to her, and then suddenly swung her around and sat her up onto the kitchen counter in clear violation of food safety regulations. Persia looked vaguely for some wet-wipes and then gave up, letting the throbbing moment — and the feeling of him pressing between her thighs — sweep her away.

A Passion for Passion

If only Sebastian could see me now . . . thought Dane, dismissing the oddly penetrating thought and returning his full focus to the luscious handful of dame on the countertop before him.

Polyamory / Ménage à Trois

THREE'S A CROWD
[Post-Apocalyptic, Polyamory, Threesome]

D'Ancey LaGuarde's Three's a Crowd *is the first in LaGuarde's new series of post-apocalyptic Romantic Fiction with unconventional pairings and a supernatural twist.*

A post-apocalyptic wasteland torn by an age-long war. A woman torn between two men. She can't have them both. Or can she?

College is a hard-bitten apocalypse scientist, immune to zombies and living in a cave near a human settlement above the ruins of what used to be New San Francisco. Life is just fine.

She's got an anti-werewolf defence fence and a ghoul-evaporating gun. She's built a secure refuge, living on canned food and VHS tapes. But the arrival of two handsome scavengers turns her world upside down.

Jace Both is an Ivy League college-professor-cum-marine, hell-bent on avenging the death of his wife. Duncan Chen is an ex-police psychoanalyst and half-werewolf who's lost everything: his pack, his home and his mind. He's only alive after Jace rescues him from a waterfall and now he's bonded to the marine. Duncan needs Jace for his sanity and in return Duncan protects Jace from his dangerously chivalrous instincts.

College reluctantly opens her home to these two dangerous men just before the monsoon blizzards shut them in for a three-month season of isolation. And soon passion simmers in every corner of the cave, and the cave is a polyhedron so that's a lot of passion.

Within the blizzard-bound security of their hidden cave, sharing resources equally, College's attraction to both Jace and Duncan sizzles in sexy dreams and in increasingly explicit Jungian campfire stories until eventually a shower accident sees her falling into Jace's thoughtful yet muscular arms.

But Duncan is suffering with his visions that can only be cured by tenderness, and their mutually repressed attractions explode into their first extremely logistical sex scene. As things between the threesome heat up, College finds herself falling for these two opposite men.

Can the men work past their differences to love her? Or would the fact that one of them is a werewolf drive her away from them and into something much more dangerous – the monsoon blizzard that no one has ever survived before but that she stomps out into after a three-way fight about who has to wash up the VHS tapes after dinner?

Unspecified Historical

LURING THE LAIRD
[Scottish, Historical]

Luring the Laird *is the fifty-third in the 'Hugs in the Hills' series of supernatural Romance Thrillers set in ancient Scotland.*

McBurnburn Castle is a formidable fortress hidden in the Highlands, shrouded in mystery and history and fog. Its thick walls hide its secrets. Western Dayre is the Earl of Craigyburn, half-English aristocrat, half-Scottish laird; he fiercely protects his Scottish heritage by frowning a lot and wearing a kilt.* And he also protects his dark secrets.

His duty is to guard the castle and its dark secrets but despite his duty, he is lonely. He has sworn to avoid the glittering parties of the London haut ton because the legendary

---

* He also hosts an international arts festival.

A Passion for Passion

Earl of Craigyburn might be cursed to live as an annually shapeshifting bear-wolf/werebear, but he doesn't need to put up with the haut ton's sneering contempt for his Scottishness even as they lust for his title. When society condemns the eccentric aristocrat for his unfriendly ways, he is cast out of even the occasional garden party and lives in the shadow of rumour and superstition wearing his kilt and skulking around his castle until someone knocks on his door late one night.

Forsythe McKenzie is the widowed daughter of the McKenzie laird, her family the traditional enemies of Craigyburn. She's a feisty Scottish thistle who seeks out the nefarious Earl of Craigyburn despite his sinister reputation. She approaches on the one night of the year when Western is in the form of a sexy bear and he fixates on her scent. She's frightened, she's furious, she's sexy, she's proposing to him and . . . she's pregnant.

He has agreed to a marriage of convenience, but refuses to touch Forsythe. To her, he seems an enigma: rough-featured but devastatingly attractive, consistently rude yet unfailingly polite, and irresistibly drawn to the daughter of his worst enemy.

There's danger in the air and something is stirring in dark places (including but not limited to his penis).

The intriguing earl is not just a captivating lover but so much more. Together they must solve the ancient enmity between their people, and the fated couple's electric connection is about to start a hidden war.

Unspecified Historical

ATHENIAN PIRATE SEXY VAMPIRE SCOUNDREL ADVENTURE
[Espionage, Stagecraft]

Athenian Pirate Sexy Vampire Scoundrel Adventure *is a new instalment from D'Ancey LaGuarde in the 'Dark Hearts of History' supernatural Romance dodecology. Strap in for another tits-out, flap-frenzying adventure by the heart-pounding author of such novels as* A Werewolf in My Sex Dungeon, Vampires of the Road Safety Department *and* A Ghoul of My Own.

*A*thenian Pirate Sexy Vampire Scoundrel Adventure is an exciting combination of action, adventure, magic, mystery, treasure hunting, seafaring, dangerous intrigue, humour and steamy romance with an exotic ancient Greek setting and enough fabulous characters to get your toga in a twist.

Sexy shameless vampire pirate scoundrel hero Melosthones loves the ladies. As a pirate vampire secret agent for the Teeth of the Amphitheatre, a secret society dedicated to protecting the world's sources of Greek mythology from the evil Furies, his primary duty is always to the mission. But if it's all in a day's work, and the success of an operation should happen to involve getting under a woman's skirt, well, that's just blood and gravy. The notorious ladies' man/vampire/pirate/theatre critic has always been able to keep things carefree, easy and aloof when it comes to the women he's attracted to. But then again, he's never encountered a woman like Mariaah.

This womanising adventurer finally meets his match in

A Passion for Passion

an intelligent, spirited priestess, and finds himself strangely and completely captivated by her. It's too bad that she's a daughter of a top member of the Teeth's sworn enemy, the Furies. Now it's up to Melosthones and some of his Teeth allies to convince expert linguist Mariaah to help translate an ancient dialect in order to find something hidden somewhere in the Greek Isles before the Furies use it for their evil aims. But Melosthones and Mariaah have an explosive attraction and magnetic chemistry that turns into a wildly passionate affair in the midst of exploration and danger. There's also a great side romance between quirky secondary characters, witch Athena and sea captain/half-merman Callus with his one fish leg and three fish fingers, whose constant bickering marks an underlying attraction.

If you like Romance with lots of action, adventure, humour, steamy love scenes, a smart plucky heroine and a to-die-for vampire pirate scoundrel hero with a heart of gold, then don't miss this highly enjoyable read.

Athenian Pirate Sexy Vampire Scoundrel Adventure, available only when you inhale the gases from the oracle of Delphi.

Unspecified Historical

LEGS IN THE GLOAMING
[Shipwreck, Stuntman]

Legs in the Gloaming *is the forty-third instalment of D'Ancey LaGuarde's violent, sexy and occasionally violently sexy 'Hell's Portico' period Romance Thriller series; a pulse-palpitating parable of two hearts torn apart by distance and brought together also by distance** *during the Golden Age of Hollywood black-and-white film.*

Bletchley is a lowly cabin girl working a cruise ship while on the run from a dark past in a small town in North Dakota. Bletchley's telepathic abilities have so far kept her a step ahead of ruin but her unusual gift attracts the attention of the very man she's trying to escape: the captain of the ship, serial douchebag, lounge singer and mass murderer known only as Captain Bloodhead.

Trapped on what was meant to be only a seven-day trip, she's cornered by the evil captain in such a sleazy way that she has no option but to run from him, setting off a series of chaotic events that accidentally sinks the ship and leaves her on the open ocean.†

Washing ashore weeks later, slightly chapped, she finds herself on a desert island with the last man on Earth she'd ever thought to see again.

---

* But the other kind of distance. The first distance is between them, and the second distance is with them together but far away from other people.

† It's okay; luckily enough all the passengers and crew on the cruise ship are also evil and deserve to die. Don't think about it too much.

A Passion for Passion

Her very survival now lies in the strong hands of her ex-best friend, dragon master and international black-and-white film stuntman Blavid, who has been abandoned by Hollywood enemies on the very same island.

They don't recognise each other at first, but the powerful pull of attraction stirs feelings they have both only felt once before . . . with each other!

Amidst the fast-talking sass, fond flashbacks and occasional full dance number, Bletchley and Blavid find themselves holding their mouths quite close together a number of times as things fade to black. A glimpse of her legs in the gloaming is all it takes to bring their troubled past and all Blavid's memories of their teen romance come roaring back like the ocean tides.

Can Bletchley forgive Blavid for breaking her heart back in high school when they were best friends harbouring mutual unrequited crushes on each other, back when he was a mere half-dragon-riding apprentice, half-gymnast, and she an orphaned but popular heiress on the cheer squad?

Will he have the strength to reveal that he only left because he thought she was too good for him and had fallen in with a Mexican dragon cartel obsessed with watching the latest Hollywood movies?* She used to be so far above him but now the tables have turned and in the hot days and steamy nights of the island they must learn to forgive the past and work

---

*   Exactly what it sounds like if you don't think too much about it and don't ask any questions.

Unspecified Historical

together to rebuild the burning passion they left behind them, and also a raft.

With the big monsoon storms coming and the next cruise ship passing by in only a few weeks, they have to write a successful film script, teach Bletchley to act on the silver screen and find the treasure of Captain Bloodhead before the international stunt council strikes Blavid from their guild and leaves him and Bletchley at the mercy of Blavid's spurned Mexican dragon cartel lover.[*]

Legs in the Gloaming is rated B for boobs. Available in all light aircraft and abandoned warehouses.

---

[*] The sinister and sexy Mariana Strenkh, who is the antiheroine and eventual love interest of the action hero Joe Gund in the Jack Reacher meets James Bond Thriller series *Jack Reacher Meets James Bond and They Talk About How Cool Joe Gund Is: A Joe Gund Adventure* by D'Ancey LaGuarde writing under the pen name of Devon Gillingham.

Christmas

Christmas is a troublesome setting for Romance, the landscape of Christmas Romance dominated by the Hallmark Christmas movie genre, in which a high-stress, big-city protagonist returns to a small town, only to fall in love with a more 'real',* less type-A life through the medium of a hot local or old flame.

But Christmas Romance can be so much more than that! The mistletoe, the snow outside, the sudden re-centring of family life are all deeply romantic, if that's your jam.† On the other hand, for many, the very homeliness of Christmas is anathema to sensuality; the rugs are too fluffy, the holly too prickly, the snow too hypothermic to lend itself to the vibrational hot slipperiness most conducive to make-out city,

---

*   Suburban authenticity, usually set in the benevolent hinterlands of America, is the most authentic kind of authenticity.

†   Christmas Romances are rarely set in Australian summer Christmas.

Christmas

you're conceptually too heavy with Christmas dinner to be uplifted by the winds of passion. The trick for a Romance author, then, is to balance the magic of Christmas with the magic of boners. When carried off successfully, a Christmas Romance can be both heart- and pants-warming.*

D'Ancey LaGuarde of course brought fresh life and new angles on the Christmas Romance genre, outraging many with the expanded 'Holiday Hotness' series, which included sexy celebrations of Diwali (*He's a God with Amnesia, She's the Nurse Who Teaches Him the Real Meaning of Inner Light*), Hanukkah (*Eight Nights by Menorah Candlelight*) and Yule (*The Yule Log*). Some of our favourites of the few which have made it over into this dimension are below.

---

* As long as nobody's wearing a Santa suit. D'Ancey's novels show a remarkable breadth of openness to the human experience of love and lust up to and including werewolf/cephalopod/sentient submarine threesomes, but D'Ancey draws the line at Santa suits. It's the fluffy white cuffs apparently.

A Passion for Passion

THE HIGHLAND LAIRD'S CHRISTMAS MIRACLE
[Scottish, Historical]

The Highland Laird's Christmas Miracle *is a super-sexy Historical period drama with a supernatural twist, set in the Highlands of history, when men were men and women were sassy Sassenachs escaping hard fates at the hands of their wicked step-half-uncles.*

Dora Pimberton is an orphaned heiress escaping a horrid Christmas fate at the hands of her wicked step-half-uncle, Lord Blightly. Escaping from his black coach in the dead of night after he spirited her to Gretna Green for a forced marriage to his loathsome son Creepington Blightly, she flees into the wet Highlands, tearing her bodice in the process.

Angus McAngus is the Laird of Loch Angus, known as the Devil Laird for his wicked eyebrows and history of violent fighting. While riding at night in a fearsome temper and mistaking Dora for a wet hussy, he sweeps her onto his magnificent stallion and angrily takes her back to his Highland castle for shenanigans.

As she explains mid-canter that she is not a hussy he respects her boundaries and restrains his massive masculine urges, which leads her to relax against him in an unbearably provocative way with her ripe bottom. Angus and Dora, surreptitiously (from each other), engage in some fraught frottage on the horse but she swoons from damp. He angrily decides that he'll never let her know that he almost came in his kilt

Christmas

from her wet butt. But when he gets her back to the castle and is confronted by her near-naked sassy Sassenachness, his heart is moved and he suggests that he rescue her ruined honour by offering her his hand in marriage.

And after she slaps him sassily in the face, he locks her in a room and goes to think it off. But she finds out from a garrulous maid that the castle is in trouble. All of his armsmen are scruffy and the local village fears the Devil Laird because of the curse that was put upon the castle once by the romantic ghost of a witch who banged his grandfather. He must marry before Christmas to break the family curse.

Dora's perky pragmatism will help these scruffy men diamond themselves out of their roughness as the sassy Sassenach breaks the curse of the Devil Laird by falling in love with him before Christmas, as the ghost witch foretold.

The Call of the Christmas Supernova

She's in disguise as a young Regency buck, but he's an alien from outer space... and it's Christmas

D'Ancey LaGuarde

Christmas

THE CALL OF THE CHRISTMAS SUPERNOVA
[Alien, Christmas, Cross-Dressing]

Thirteenth in LaGuarde's Regency Christmas alien vampire series, 'Sleigh Slay Stay', The Call of the Christmas Supernova *is a Historical Romance with a supernatural extraterrestrial twist.*

Set in the wet streets of an almost-Regency London, *The Call of the Christmas Supernova* is a heartwarming tale of a grinchy vampire alien prince and the brilliant yet vulnerable duchess who heals his horrible heart.

Stranded in more-or-less Regency London after the crash of his interstellar vampire ship and the destruction of all his people in the recent supernova wars, Lothien assumes the identity of a man about town and goes around to all the gambling clubs playing Faro and resisting the urge to drink the blood of his colleagues. When he saves a genteel young man in distress from a mugging by thugs, he succumbs to the flashing passion in the man's unlikely violet eyes and rescues him away to his country villa.

The young man is in fact Claridia, an orphaned duchess escaping the tyrannical rule of the horrible trustees who wish only to marry her to the worst possible man, Earl Witherington, a smelly rake with gout and perversions.

She has disguised herself as a man in order to win herself back at cards from Witherington, but when he challenges her to a gun duel, she is only too grateful to accept the help of a mysteriously sharp-toothed gentleman. Trapped by pre-Christmas snows in Lothien's luxurious villa, she begins to uncover his space secrets as he begins to awaken her secret sexiness.

When she loses her shirt in a mistletoe accident, simultaneously revealing her creamy breasts and her sexy cross-dressing secret, Lothien must nobly kiss her according to ancient mistletoe law.

But he is tormented by a dark secret: if he engages in full alien to human lovemaking with anyone, he must immediately eat them unless they're his one true love and it's Christmas, which among his alien vampire people is a special day also but not for the same reasons.

But if he *doesn't* make love this Christmas, he will die.

Claridia must win the esteem of this passionate prince before the clock strikes midnight on Christmas Eve, saving both of their lives with the promise of a future.

The Call of the Christmas Supernova is available at all gift-wrapping counters and pop-up dollar-store festive-décor outlets.

Quizzes

Some people just can't enjoy something unless they win.
D'ANCEY LAGUARDE

If the goal of this book is to make you feel good about Romance, some of you will need to be assured that Romance is a legitimate form of art. There is no better way to comfort people than to assert that there is an objective truth in the universe, and the best way to do that is by setting a multiple choice quiz.

A Passion for Passion

QUIZ 1

1. In *The Earl-ish Duke's Half-Hungarian Headmistress,* what is the Earl of Duke's vow after his disastrous marriage?

   A) Never to return to England
   B) Never to become a schoolteacher
   C) Never to succumb to the temptation of love again
   D) Never to break the haunted vase that contains the spirit of his ex-wife
   E) Never to go up against a Sicilian when death is on the line

2. What supernatural element is featured in *The Wicked Wastrel?*

   A) Vampire landlords, driven to suck the life out of you and also charge you rent
   B) Ghosts who are summoned every time the protagonist is tumescent
   C) Werewolf lawyers conveyancing radioactive land
   D) A family curse of sleep-thievery and night-kleptomania
   E) A long-lost prophecy enclosed for centuries in a puzzle box

Quizzes

3. In *Excavating Her Passion*, what is Fox's disgrace related to?

- A) Running away with a married woman
- B) Stealing dinosaur bones from the British Museum and returning them to their families*
- C) Refusing a duel by being too honourable to fight the brother of the meaningless mistress he was sleeping with at the time
- D) Eating a dumpling too large for a human man
- E) Being a fox

4. What is the main conflict for Cassandra in *Down for the Count*?

- A) Her bird curse
- B) The dyslexia that haunts her family lion
- C) Her distant father's gambling habit
- D) Her inability to trust men with brown hair
- E) Her heaving breasts consistently throwing her off balance so she falls over

---

* Now mostly chickens.

5. In *The Dragon Lord's Lady,* what secret does Balentheon reveal to Salexandra?

A) He is the bastard son of a bastard
B) He is a dragon
C) He is a king
D) He is a dragon king
E) He is the bastard son of the dragon king

Answers

C) Never to succumb to the temptation of love again
D) A family curse of sleep-thievery and night-kleptomania
A) Running away with a married woman
A) Her bird curse
E) He is the bastard son of the dragon king

Quizzes

QUIZ 2

1. **In *The Piercing Falcon*, what curse prevents Garwin from returning to the fae court?**

    A) A curse from a rival fae
    B) A curse from his jealous stepfather
    C) A curse from a hedge-witch ex-lover
    D) A self-imposed curse

2. **What is the unique feature of Persia in *The SEALs' Sexy Seal*?**

    A) She is a half-seal, sexy on both land and water
    B) She has wings, but only on Saturdays
    C) She can read minds but only if she reads out loud
    D) She is an ex-circus performer whose circus was burned down by Batman

3. **Who are the two individuals Hadrian falls in love with in 'The Lost Duke's Last Loves'?**

    A) A fae princess and a sassy maid
    B) A bisexual industrialist and a disgraced courtesan
    C) A childhood friend and a new frenemy
    D) A tormented fellow noble and a debonair foreign dignitary

4. In *The Dim Menagerie*, what dual identity does Devin hold?

   A) Half-vampire, half-Victorian doctor
   B) Half-werewolf, half-hard-boiled detective
   C) Half-noble wizard, half-sleazy close-up card-trick magician
   D) Half-wizard, half-eggman, one-third walrus

5. What is Violet's condition when Devin first meets her in *The Dim Menagerie*?

   A) She is musically blind: incapable of perceiving musical instruments even when they're right in front of her
   B) She has an anachronistic vocabulary, an elasticated corset . . . and amnesia. She doesn't need a man but she can't remember why
   C) She is haunted by the bankruptcy of an ill-fated pop-up skincare stall that failed on launch because it was hundreds of years before its time
   D) She has a curse that causes her to faint at the sight of abs

Quizzes

Answers

- C) A curse from a hedge-witch ex-lover
- A) She is a half-seal, needing both land and water
- B) A bisexual industrialist and a disgraced courtesan
- A) Half-vampire, half-Victorian doctor
- B) She has an anachronistic vocabulary, an elasticated corset . . . and amnesia. She doesn't need a man but she can't remember why

Afterword

BY D'ANCEY LAGUARDE

I have never given commentary on any of my books to this date; I believe texts ought really to speak for themselves. Which is to say, anything I'd like to say for a book, I'd like to think I'd already said with the book.

In an age where many find it impossible to separate the artist from the art, I have cut out the middle-person and made of myself an enigma.

Nothing is publicly known about my private life, nor about the childhood that led me to fame as the most best-selling online Romance maven in the history of mixed-genre romantico-physical depictions of the human condition (that happen often to provide heavy representation of skilful fingering) and I like it that way.

This book has not therefore been filled with adorable anecdotes about my precocious childhood, tours of my luxurious home, revelations about my troubled private life or, God

Afterword

forbid, my opinions on politics. It has instead, by my insistence, been focused on the books themselves.

May I request, should any readers encounter me on my morning constitutional, clad in my walking garb of tweed capelet, knee-high boots and aerodynamic sun-monocle, that they continue calmly on their way without asking me to pose for anything or sign any of their bits. I ask that you be grateful perhaps, for the moment of serendipity that brought our paths together, but containing, if you can, within your hearts the seed of letting go which characterises all true and pure admiration.

Fan art is always welcome, photographs are not. I am told an ancestor of mine was a cryptid, a family myth I can neither verify nor deny, but it is true that I don't show up on digital or physical film or in some mirrors. There is quite a good oil painting of me on a mantel somewhere, but I've forgotten where, and apparently it fails to turn out novels at exactly the inverse of the pace at which mine emerge, so best not to interfere, one feels.

That said, there comes a time in every great author's life where one begins to turn one's mind to legacy, and to reflecting on some of the extraordinary achievements of a life spent creating. In my time as a groundbreaking and genre-penetrating creator, I have built worlds of words. Writing and publishing at a rate of approximately one book every four to five days for many decades has given me a back catalogue of such enormity that this work can only lightly and tenderly touch upon its farthest margins like a smitten youth on a ballroom dancefloor.

A Passion for Passion

I have writ words that have moved people to passion, laughter, tears ... deeply unrealistic ideas about what healthy relationships might look or sound like. If I had ever shared my address, I know I would have been swamped by the gratitude of the public just as the loins of any number of my heroes and heroines have been swamped by their deep-held but long-denied feelings towards any number of lords, lairds, servants, captains of industry, elves, muscular aliens, half-dragon/half-budget travel advisory board members and octopods. But I need no thanks! It is sufficient for me to be a bestselling phenomenon of staggering magnitude, live in my palatial abode, have enough money to keep me in aerodynamic sun monocles and to never publish my opinions about anything online.

I know I've shaped more than one generation's urges, for better or worse, towards a life more full of risk, reward and horseback-based erotic declarations of esteem, and for that I can only be truly grateful to the reading public who have supported me through time and across dimensions. And to demonstratively answer the perennial question of whether I exist or not, I say now: 'Can anybody be said to exist as an artist without their audience?' Truly, it is you, the reader (who is reading this now), who makes me real.

Fashion Tips

BY D'ANCEY LAGUARDE

It is a truism that on the internet, nobody knows you're a dog. And when you're a mysterious figure simultaneously dominating the self-published Romance market and also concealing every fact about your private life from the ravening hordes, nobody knows for sure that you're not a dog. While I will neither confirm nor deny whether I'm not a dog, I will say that over my long professional life of describing clothes being taken off, fumbled under or rubbed through while on horseback, I have developed some strong opinions on fashion.

The following are some of my best fashion tips for writers, readers and the illiterate mutants who will be reciting this uncomprehendlingly as oral history to one another over a bin fire in the not-too-distant future (I salute you with as many hands as is appropriate and hope to serve you all as a potential market segment).

A Passion for Passion

While some may say it doesn't matter what you wear when you're a self-published Romance maven, I say if you want my job, you might as well dress for it.

1. The Writing Cape: Versatility Meets Elegance

The writing cape is a staple in my wardrobe. It's not only stylish but also incredibly versatile, and can even be worn outdoors in a pinch, though I do have a soft spot for my specialised Harris tweed outdoor walking cape with its mouthpiece for inflation, as well as a light and a whistle for attracting any attention that you haven't already attracted by wearing a cape.

Tips for Wearing a Cape:

- **Choose the Right Length:** A knee-length cape offers freedom of movement while still providing ample coverage. An ankle-length cape is more modest but can be a trip hazard. Short, thigh-length capes are for sluts, so bear that in mind as the optimal choice if you are planning a night on the town. Anything shorter than thigh length is barely deserving of the name cape and might as well be called a shawl.

- **Fabric Matters:** Opt for materials like lightweight wool for cooler climates or a breathable cotton blend for warmer weather. Polyester capes are

Fashion Tips

prone to pilling and can be a fire hazard. It's worth investing in quality materials, lest you look like a capely-come-lately or a halloween draculist.

- **Accessorise Smartly:** Pair your cape with a belt for a cinched look or let it flow freely for a more dramatic effect, depending on whether you prefer to leave the room by walking or by swirling out in the midst of a cloud of smoke.*

2. The Aerodynamic Sun Monocle: Function and Flair

Unlike a trad monocle an aerodynamic sun monocle isn't just for reading or sneering at those beneath you or assessing stolen jewels – it's a statement piece that adds a touch of intellectual allure.

Tips for Incorporating a Monocle:

- **Proper Fit:** Ensure your monocle fits comfortably. It should rest securely in your socket. Never ever resort to monocle glue. It is the last resort of a desperate soul. Monocle gestures should always be meaningful, never nervous.

---

* Check smoke and vaping regulations in your area.

- **Style Variations:** Choose a monocle with a subtle chain for a classic look or go chainless for a more modern, sleek appearance.

- **Occasion Matters:** While prescription lenses are perfect for formal events, intellectual gatherings or brisk walks, reserve their use for when your depth perception is of secondary importance. Never during sword fights.

3. Charms and Sigils

My mother always refused to buy t-shirts with writing on them, seeing it as an uncouth practice. I am generally in agreement but make an occasional exception for protective spellwork and arcane runes.

Tips for Incorporating Charms and Sigils:

- **Embroidered Symbols:** Embroidering mystical symbols onto your clothing can be both protective and fashionable, but beware of cheap spells from shonky practitioners. Online retailers that promise cheap spells delivered right to your home sound too good to be true, and that's because they are. They won't last, and they will smell weird when they arrive.

Fashion Tips

- **Tailored Spells:** An ethically tailored spell from a local maker will make you look chic and proportionate, as well as fend off any lurking attack magic or demonic possession, and you'd be surprised by how reasonable the prices are.

4. Practical Pockets

Pockets are a kind of little bag that's either sewn into your garment or attached with buttons, strings or grommets. Whether you're wearing a casual wetsuit, full-body armour or a pair of shorts, make sure you have enough pockets for all your needs. As a writer, I always use my pockets to carry a notebook and a pen, along with a few other essentials such as mace for discouraging attackers, a mace of the mediaeval type for discouraging attackers and the spice known as mace for when you might suddenly have to cook for a band of bandits who have just kidnapped you on the road.

Tips for Pockets:

- **Hidden Pockets:** Incorporate hidden pockets into your garments for a sleek look.

- **Hidden Hidden Pockets:** If putting things into a pocket would ruin the line of your cape, try a pocket dimension. Infinitely flexible, the pocket dimension is portable, stylish and only occasionally creates a black hole in your pants.

A Passion for Passion

5. Personal Signature Style

Above all, your fashion should reflect your unique personality. By incorporating these tips, you can bring a touch of Fantasy and Romance to your wardrobe, ensuring you stand out in any dimension.

Tips for Creating Your Signature Style:

- **Identify Key Elements:** Determine the key elements that define your style, whether it's a particular colour palette, accessory or your familiar enchanted animal who needs a reinforced shoulder pad to sit on.*

- **Be Bold:** Don't be afraid to experiment with bold patterns or unusual accessories. Extra limbs, a time machine, a sentient axe, all of those can scream, and if you can make out what they're screaming, you'll find it's often 'Fashion!'

- **Stay Authentic:** Your style should be an authentic representation of who you are, so wear what makes you feel confident and comfortable in your sense of self.

---

* The reinforced shoulder pad does not work if your Familiar is a horse or manatee.

Encountering Romance

I can remember my first time encountering Romance novels. We had a junk room in our house where the lightbulb was forever broken. We called it the dark room. Up on the top of a cupboard at the back of the room there was a cardboard box, and in front of the cupboard was a pile of old mattresses that we used to play on as kids. I can't remember the impulse that took me to climb a mattress to the top of the cupboard, but I can remember sliding back down with the heavy box on my lap, and opening it up in the shaft of light from the door to reveal the glitter of book covers.

My mum always said Romance books were like sweets and so she would cover them with the wrappers from easter eggs, and then with plastic contact film, so they felt precious and special and secret, and like they had been loved.

I assumed later that it was also to conceal the lurid clinch covers from people who might judge my intellectual giant of a mother for such seemingly frivolous reading material.

I was probably too young for some of the more pulsating

A Passion for Passion

scenes in the novels but I was an avid reader, and my mum operated on the basic principle that reading was inherently virtuous (certainly more virtuous than TV), so instead of watching kid-friendly game shows or teen Disneyverse comedies, I was given free rein to read Rumpole and Anne McCaffrey, Georgette Heyer, Gene Wolfe and Dostoevsky.

Later in life, of course, with *The Last Post*[*] and the opening of the Glitch in the Space-Time Continuum™, D'Ancey LaGuarde's works made their way into this dimension and eventually into this book. I am so grateful to the dark room, to the pile of mattresses and to my mother's secret stash of guilty-pleasure reading, for the seeds it planted in me that have grown into this book.

Welcome to the works of D'Ancey, and into the magnificent world that I hope, through the course of this book, I have invited you.

---

[*] *The Last Post* was a podcast set in an alternate dimension hosted by an alternate version of myself. We ran ads, and I felt weird about doing ads, so I thought about what I'd feel comfortable advertising, and the rest is history, or historical fiction set in an alternate dimension posing as satire while in part being satire about satire. With a supernatural twist.

But Is D'Ancey LaGuarde Real?

I have been asked to admit that this is a book about an author who doesn't exist. I have been asked — as the only person who has been able to communicate directly across the interdimensional boundaries to bring D'Ancey's work into this world — whether D'Ancey LaGuarde is a fictional character, a figment of my own imagination.*

---

* Nice. In wrestling, the term 'kayfabe' is used to mean a sort of layer cake of fourth wall, in which wrestlers maintain their on-stage storylines in front of outsiders or the media. The blurred lines of awareness about and consent to and being in on these storylines make for a heady soup where fans can messily and excitingly feel invested in maintaining the illusions of the world and accepting the reality of those illusions. The first public acknowledgment by a major insider of the staged nature of professional wrestling came in 1989 when the owner of the World Wrestling Federation (and character within it) Vince McMahon (if that is his real name) testified before the New Jersey State Senate that wrestling was not a competitive sport. Since then, wrestling fans have been in an era of 'neo-kayfabe' in a post-ironic world, which may or may not involve a performance of a second layer of selfhood for the fans.

A Passion for Passion

But let's pretend for a moment that D'Ancey LaGuarde is not really such a powerhouse of self-published novelistic success that the works have achieved a quantum force that has broken through the barriers between dimensions into our own. Let's pretend that D'Ancey is a joke taken too far. Imagine we'd written an entire book about someone and managed never to decide or reveal by a careless pronoun whether D'Ancey is a man, a woman or even human.

Would you rather live in that world? Or would you rather live in the world of this book, where D'Ancey LaGuarde can, at the rate of about once a week, bring you a new excursion into the world of passion, forbidden adventure, heaving bosoms, palpitating wallflowers, horny dragons, make-out-based-destiny and noble guard captains whose white knuckles tighten on the handles of their swords as they manfully restrain their burning longing for the princesses that they have sworn to protect?

I'd rather live in the world of this book where D'Ancey LaGuarde is real. Because to write an entire book dedicated to celebrating the extensive works of an author I made up would be an extreme commitment to silliness in the name of nothing more than celebrating the stupid things that make us happy. And who'd read that?!

Academic Thoughts on Mystery

BY DR DOCTOR PROFESSOR FRUMPSBY
VON GRUNTLEBUNK, PHD, MD,
MA, MSCI, BPHIL (HONS)

Unfortunately for D'Ancey scholars, while the works themselves are prolific, the person (Man? Woman? NB? Co-op? Alien? Sentient matrix? Octopusperson?) is mysterious.

It is posited that D'Ancey's refusal to be constrained by the subgenres of the genres in which the LaGuarde books are written is a manifestation of an obsession in the author with liminal spaces. Such a claim is supported by the number of times LaGuarde protagonists find themselves operating outside society, or engaging in sensual encounters in hallways, doorways, tunnels, cellars, horseback and in the space beyond space while time-travelling.

The approach of the books to genre is also supportive of such a hypothesis. Rarely does D'Ancey LaGuarde operate

A Passion for Passion

within the strict confines of a specific form: plain Romance or Fantasy or Science Fiction. Instead, it's the hyphenated genres: Historico-Mysterious, Science-Fictionally-Sexual, Action-Adventure-Romance and, of course, the with-a-supernatural-twists. If there can be said to be a stamp of such a prolific and wide-ranging author, it is in the relentless straddling of subgenre, of genre and (for the protagonists) of each other.

Psychiatrists suggest that this 'outsiding the box' of definition is possibly a response to childhood bullying or an expression of liminal self-identity, though given the scarcity of biographical material it is impossible for a scholar to confirm or deny this hypothesis. The best kind of hypothesis, if internet celebrities are to be believed.*

Of course, for modern academia, in the lacuna that is D'Ancey's identity, it is difficult to know how to measure and value the achievements and contributions of the works to the field of Romance, Mystery, Science Fiction and Historico-supernatural bang-fests.

If D'Ancey were a woman writing for women, that would have very different implications than if D'Ancey were not a woman, but some other non-woman type of person. What then can we imagine if D'Ancey were one day unmasked as an Octopus Person!? Could society deal with the knowledge of how truly and repeatedly such a being has connected to the deep human desire to be chastely yet heatedly riding across an agrarian landscape, buttock to crotch with their beloved,

---

* They're not.

on horseback? How could an Octopus Person know so much about the sociopolitical and emotional impact of fingering in a culture of sexual repression?

Perhaps then, despite our curiosity, it is better for us not to know. Moreover, in the modern age of data transparency it must be applauded that we have at least one public figure who has managed to remain truly private.

Romance is a genre mostly written by women and for women; historically undervalued for that very reason, but a genre that almost by definition has a fully formed female character at its centre, whose concerns and desires are pivotal to the movement and resolution of the plot. Of course, with the rise of queer Romance, many more kinds of people and relationship types are finding their ways into Romance, but the shadow of the genesis of the genre remains imprinted in its DNA.

There are perennial tensions in Romance between centring and valuing feminine desires and the ways in which such books – through wish fulfilment – can replicate or reinforce problematic norms. The distinction between escapism from a less than perfect world and the cultivation of unrealistic ideas about the number of abs a man can feasibly have must be made and maintained, lest such books become toxic to the very people who self-medicate with them. We must all as readers hold ourselves responsible for maintaining perspective on the amount of after that happily can ever be, lest we spend our time comparing ourselves unfavourably with a half-vampire, half-leopard, half-underwear model.

As D'Ancey LaGuarde (but no D'Ancey LaGuarde heroine ever) says: 'Sometimes it's not that deep.'

Postscript

Thank you for coming to the end of this book.

The 'companion to a famous author's work' is a genre that I would liken to the bag salad of books. Like bag salad, 90 per cent of which is bought aspirationally and then binned uneaten, I think people buy this kind of book more than they read it. And let's be honest, they don't buy it that often.

The companion book is the gift for an uncle who you know likes Batman, or the tongue-in-cheek legal writings of Alfred Thompson 'Tom' Denning, Baron Denning, OM, PC, DL, or Jeeves and Wooster or Harry Potter. It's bought as a way of saying, 'I know you, Uncle! I know the things you like!' and received in a similarly friendly spirit. It then sits on a shelf, making a complete collection superfluously complete.

It's the hat on a hat of authorial fandom, and I'd like to reiterate that although I'm so glad you've bought this book, I have put myself under some pressure to make it the kind of book you can actually read and enjoy. Though you have already given me your money or somehow acquired this book

Postscript

through nefarious means or friendship, I'd take it in a kindly spirit if you would consider recommending this to friends or frenemies or online or the other places one can recommend things. If you didn't like it, I should mention now that it's too late, you've finished the book and also that I don't process returns; all D'Ancey LaGuarde-related books count like underpants and swimwear from department stores. It is impossible to render them clean once purchased. They must be considered soiled by use, lest we communicate infections.

Thanks go to Henry Fraser, Tom Clutterbuck, Steffan Alun Gwen, Greg, all the good people at Unbound, every listener to Bugleverse shows, all my patreon subscribers, Maria Eduarda Guillerme dos Santos, Holly Rose Heather Wood.

Chris Skinner, Ped Hunter, for notes, reassurance and moral and ethical and practical support.

And to PB. Always.

Unbound is a publisher which champions bold, unexpected books.

We give readers the opportunity to support books directly, so our authors are empowered to take creative risks and write the books they really want to write. We help readers to discover new writing they won't find anywhere else.

We are building a community in which authors engage directly with people who love what they do. It's a place where readers and writers can connect with and support one another, enjoy unique experiences and benefits, and make books that matter.

This book is in your hands because readers made it possible. Everyone who pledged their support is listed below. Join them by visiting unbound.com and supporting a book today.

Supporters

Thomas A
Laura Abbott
Daniel Abrams
Coralie Acheson
Lauren Ackerley
Megan Ackerman-Yost
John Acock
Alexander Adam
Beth Adamowicz
Julia Adams
Josh Addison
Michael Aguilar
Stefan Aichhorn
Alapan
Craig Aldridge
Owen Alexander
John Alford
Peter Alfred
Alice is a star
Graham Allan
Annie Allen
Dave Allen
Simon Allen
Tim Allen
James Allenspach
Charles Allport
Emily Allwright
Gabe Alpert, Nikka Rosenstein
Yasamin Amirabadi

Amnon Amos
Ann Anderson
Michael Anderson
Peter Andreae
Matthew Andreoli
Andrew <3
Anitha & Sridhar Vesselina Araptcheva
Dominic Archer
David Arkless
Fareed Armaly
Arran
Ian Arwas
Peter Ash
Ash, you are my Secret History Professor
LauraEllen Ashcraft
Max Ashford
Valerie Askin
Paul Aurich
Benjammin Austin
D'Alice Avey
William Axford
Ben Ayliffe
Victor Azevedo
A B
Andrew B
Ben B
Georgi Badakhshan

Brian Baer
Michael Baer
Jaskaran Bahia
Martin Baines
Phil Baines
Joe Baker
Sally Baker
Baldie
Tom Banks
Cassidy Barkalow
Dave Barker
Rick Barnard
H Kevin Barnes
Emma Bartholomew
Dave Bartos
Michele Bartos
Sara Basturk
Richard Batstone
Nicole Battafarano
Seth Battis
Nathan Bauer
Alison Bazylinski
Gregory Bear, Charlotte Linda Armstrong-Gilbert
Alex Beasley
Chad Beaver
Timothy Beaver
Charles Behorney
M'Artin Belderson

Supporters

Aaron & Stephanie Bell
Donald Belly
Darren Bennett
Hannah Bennett
Richard Bennett, Kirsty Merryn
Layne Benofsky
Aaron Bentley
Alan Bentley
Jay Berkes
Liz Berman
Matthew Berry
Richard Berzé
John Besford
Paul Best
Tomaž Bešter
Deniz Bevan
Christ Bingo
Graham Bird
James Bird
Matt Bishop
Lee Biskin
Jan Blabla
C. E. Blackledge
David Blair
Carrie Blake
Ciorstan Blake
Sadie Rocketship Blake
Marissa Blank
Michael Blank, Liz Brooks
Amanda Bligh, PhD
Jonathan Block
David Bloomquist
Nick Bodinet
Maddy Bognar
Skylar Bohan
Breanne Boland
Rachael Bolger
Daniel Boline
David Bone
Katherine Bono
David Book
Greg Borgartz
Paul Bostwick
Fitz Bowen
Melissa Bowers
Carl Boyd
Felicity Boyd
Maureen Boyle
Catherine Braiding
Kevin Brake
Jimmy Bramante
Anne Brander
Aaron Bratcher, Roy Bratcher
Daniel Bray
Colm Brennan
Peter Brennan
Van Brenner, Alfonzo Flarinky, Jesus
H. Richard M. Nixon Christ, VBinNV, F***
You Chris
Bill Brereton
Ariel Brestin
Casey Briggs
Shaun Briggs
Jon Bright
Vaughn Britton
Ian Brodie
Jonathan Broughton-Humphries
Christopher Brown
J M Brown
John Brown
Josh Brown
Lesley Brown
Lucinda Brown
Simon Brown
Vicky Brown
Amelia Brownstein
Beth Brumbaugh
Isambard Kingdom Brunel
Nick Bryan
Robert Bryson
Daniel Buchanan
Simon Buckmaster
Annedrew Budaueri

Supporters

Zoe Budd
Jeff Bull
Robert Burclaff
George P. Burdell
Tom Burger
Matthew Burgess
Brian Burke
Megan Burke
Tucker Burleigh
Elizabeth Burlingame
Ann Burlingham
Joe Burnham
Christopher Burns
Christopher Burns
David Burns
Mark Burrell
Joanne Burrows
Brian Burston
Paul Burton
Michael Butler
Robin Butterhof
Richard Byrnes
Jamie C
Justin C
Zachary Cahn
Roxanne Cahn
Ves Cain
Michael Caines
Daniel Cairns
Nicholas Campagna
Sean Campbell
Christopher Cannell
Rohan Cannon
Seth Carbon
Andrew Cardwell
A Carey
Michelle Carlson
Ginger, Carmen
Chris Carr
Colette Carroll
Simon Carroll
Georgia Carson
Antony Carter
Quinlan Cartmell-Martin
Greg Carty-Hornsby
Alex Cascone the tromboner
M. G. Case
Chris Cash
David Caso
Imogen Cassidy
Kiran Castellino
Daniel Catchpole
Caz
Joe Ceirante
Christopher Ceron
Kasia Chadwick
Tina Chaffee
Sudhakar Chandra
Trevor Chapman
Alan Charlton
Kevin Charlton
Lizzie Chase
Janet Chen
Kelly Childress
Scott Chisholm
Chochmolog
Agata Chomicz
Rachel Choo
Daniel Christensen
Sarah Christianson
Kim Chrono Detective
Meagan Cihlar
Eli Cizewski-Robinson
John Claridge
James Clarke
Audrey Class
Peter Clausen
Nelson Clayton
Stuart Clear
Harry Cobbold
Adrian Cockcroft
Mark Cohen
Melanie Cohen
Sophy Colbert
Alex Colcombe
Kermit Cole
Kofi Coleman & Ceri Evans
Linda Coletta
David Collier
Francesca Collins

Supporters

Matt Collins
Matthew Collins
Helen Comerford
Filipe Condessa
Mark Cook
Margaret Cooke
Caroline Cooper
Randal Cooper
David Cooper,
  Meghan Cooper
Sarah Corrigan
Nuno Costa
Ian Cotterill
Richard Cotton
Keith Cowans
Debbie Cowens
Wind Cowles
Steven Cox
Martin Coyle
Marquis Th.
  Craven
Paul Crawford
Rowan Crawford
Sam Cresswell
David Critics
Stephen Cromwell
Martin Cron
Daniel Maxell
  Crosby
Mark Crossley
Douglas Crovo
Gábor Csekey
CSV
Daniel Cullen
Christopher
  Culp
David Cure
Jules Curran
John Curtis
George Cusack
Karl Custer
Sean D
Pete D'Oubtfire
Andrew Daborn
Hester Dade
Christian Frey
  Dahl
James Daily
Josie Dallam
Craig Dalton
Julian Danton
Tomi Dapshi
Alexandra
  Josephine
  Darbyshire
Dean Darley
Diganta Das
Benjamin
  Davenport, Lord
  Herring De
  Boner
Gareth David
Alistair Davidson
Glenn Davidson
Daval Davis
James Davis
Mark Davis
Chris Day
Michael Day
Rob Day
William Day
Robert de Niet
Karen DeBortoli
Jason Dehlinger
Mark Deluca
Boryana Deniker
Nick Denny
Dwight Deuring
Isabella Deutsch
Linda Diamond
Elizabeth Dibble
Brian Dignam
Tim DiLauro
Ms. Phyllis
  Diller
Christopher
  Dionne
Doug Dixon
Thomas
  Domingo
Harri Donaie
Louise Dore
Kelly Doudna
Paul Douglas
Frank Dowsett
Alexander
  Patrick Doyle
  - The Marquis
  D'Carabas

Supporters

Matt Draddy
Paul Drake
Drew
Paul Dreyer
Jacques du Plessis
El Duderino
Iona Dudley
Monsignor the Rev. Pud Dudley
Chris Duerden
Barbara Dunlap
Tony Dunmore
Michael Eland Dunn
Andy Dunsmore
Catherine Dy
John Dyer
J E
Benedict E-W
Tony Eaglestone
Steve Eames
Ken Eckman
Cuzn Ed
Michael Edelstein
Claire Edgar
Kristen Edgar
Richard Edlin
Keith Edwards
Rubyanna Edwards, Sam Dennis
Rachel Ehrlich
Jonathan Eigen
Anna Helander Ekberg
James Elder
Brad Elliott
Judith Elliott
Rob Ellis
Sedrina Ellis
Bill Ellison
Christopher Ellison
Ember
The Enavs
Ian Erasmus
Lucas Erler
Erik Escobedo
Nick Escow
Michael Espinos
Michael Essex
David Estall
J. Evan Gravitt
David Anthony Evans
Peter Evans
Rebecca Evans
Eylan Ezekiel
Mark Fanshawe
Miklós Farkas
Shirley Farnham
Algenon Farquaad
Adam Farrell
Carolina Corbalán Faura
Krista Feick
Daniel Feild
Tom Ferguson
Peter Fermoy
Kelly Ferris
Fetket
Matthew Fiehn
Richard Field
Andrew Fielder
Edward Fielding
Lt. Col. Edward B. Fienning
James Fingleton
Doug Fingliss, Erin McEntee
Steve Finney
Charles Firth
Tom Fitz-Hugh
Mira Fitzsimons
Amy Flaming
William Flanigan
Ben Flatley
Holly Flint
Gaynol Flora
Steve Flower
Kevin Foad
Zoe Foley
Pedro Fonseca
Lila Fontes
Anne Ford
Andrew Forrest
Matt Forrest
James Forrester

Supporters

Eric Foster
Rob Foster
Matt Fowler
Doctor FQ,
  Anonymous
  Luria
Jay Francis
Valerie Francis
Kirsten Franklin
Kostia Franklin
Adam Fraser
Henry Fraser
Jessica Fredkin
Willa Freedman
Andy Freeman
Nancy Freeman
Harry & Lily
  French
Jeffrey Freymann
Matthew Fried
Eric Frome
Caroline Fu
Lily Fullegar-
  Cooper
Owen Fulton
Rodney Funk
Shingo Furukawa
T. Chucky G.
Brendan Gosling
  Gage
Rose Galbraith
Olivier Galletti
Chris Gantner

Paul Gardiner
Andrew Garrett,
  Sally-Anne
  Wherry
Doug Garside
Andy Gass
J. J. Gass
David Gassaway
Gaston and Biddy
James Gay
Steve Geier
Sally Elizabeth
  George, David
  Jeremiah Joseph
  George
Joanna Geralyn
Glen Germaine
Jon Gerrard
Lindsey Getson
Karen Gibbs
Monica Gibbs
Katie Gibson
Richard Gibson
Bryn Gilbertson
Gwen Gillingham
  and Bethany
  Keffala
Princess Snicker
  Ginger, Meow
  Meow Mittens
Corey Gingerich
Anthony Giorgi
Mim Glasby

Robin Glithro
Goatface
Jonnie Godfrey
David Goffin
S. Goldstine
Nihar Gondalia
Alex Gonzalez
Ian Good
Aaron Goodisman
Douglas Gordon
Hugh Gordon
Sam Gordon
Jamie Gortmaker
Monica Goswick
Ros Gough
João Graça
Daniel Grace
Simon Graf
Della Kate
  Graham
Tom Graham
Damien Grainger
Scott Grandi-Hill
Alexander Gray
Aaron Green
Hillary Green-
  Lerman
Rafael Leon
  Greenblatt
Lincoln Greenhaw
Logan Grieser
Quinn Griffin
Stuart Griffith

Supporters

Simon Griffiths
Kevin Griggs
Morgan Grubb
Miles Grubbs
Maximilian Grundke
Michael Guerriero
Anders Gustafsson
David Gustavsen
Kim Gusway
Kenny Guy
John H.
Angie Hagan
Jacob Haller
Joseph Hallett
Matthew Hambley
Steve Hameister
Doug Hanke
Hankins
Kate Hannington
Evan Hanover
Sam Hansen
Mo Hanson
Slate Hardbody
Sarah Harding
Michael Hardy
Ralf Haring
David Harper
Josh Harriman
Crispin Harris
Erik W. Harris
Ian Harris
Patrick Harris
Paul Harris
Chris Harrison
Ali Hart
Megan Hart
Dan Hartigan
Ed Hartley
Max Harvey
Rick Harvey
Eva Hasa
Wisam Hasan
Douglas Haun
John J Hayes
Sasha Hayes-Rusnov
David Haymes
John Haynes
Sherri Hayward
Daniel Hayward-Hughes
Chris Hazell
Lexi Headrick
Martin Healy
Hefin
Joseph Helbing
Kendall Helland
David Heming
Tom Hemmings
Chris Hemsley
Peter Henderson
Benjamin Hendy
Mark Herbaugh
Annika Herbert
Elizabeth Heritage
Fabian Hermann
Cort Heroy
Lena Hesselgrave
Craig Hewitt
Ele Heys
Melinda Hileman
Zita Hill, Mallory Eagles
Abigail Hillen
Hadyn Hitchins
Drs HLG
Chris Hoare
David Hochhausen
Ryan Hodges
Alex Hoffmann
Simon Jon Sørensen Høgh
Jacob Høigilt
Amelia Hoisington
Andy Hole
Steve Holland
Charlotte Hollingsworth
Ruben Homan
Paula Hope
Martin Hopkins
Nick Hornby
Jessica Hornsby
Gregory Horowitz
Rebecca Horowitz
Ian Horsey

Supporters

Tod Hostetler
Matthew Hothersall
Shaobo Hou
Gregory House
Ruairidh Howells
Julie Hsieh
Lorenz Huber
Helen Hubert
Barry Hudson
Martin Huggon
JP Hughes\:
  Thane of Cascadia
Jani Hukka
Keith Humphreys
Rik Humphreys
Matthew Hunt
Keith Hurley
Anders Hurtig
Lachlan Hutton
Chris Hyland
Marten I
Bearded Ian
M G Ibbs
Debora Iera
Dan Ilic
Christopher Inman
Alexis Irvin
Stephen "Badger" Isaac
Salimah Ismail

Emily Ivie
Pendaran Iwys
E J
Huweth J'Ohnathan III
Elizabeth Jackman
Lee Jackrel
Jon Jacobs
Isaiah Jacques
Davin Jaehne
Aabra Jaggard
Franz Jahnke
Nicholas Jainschigg
Alexander Jameson
Ellen Jameson
David C Jay
Adrian Jenkin
Bruncle Jo
Rich John
Ivan Johnson
Peter Johnson
Sandra Johnson
Jonathan
Andrew Jones
Charlotte Walker Jones
Darrin Jones
Ewan Jones
Keith Jones
Mark Jones
Phil Jones
Sally Jones

Carl J Jonsson
Paul Jonusaitis
Jason Jooste
Kolin Jordan
Omkar Joshi
Jundar
Lucas Jurkovic
Ray Kachel
Michael Kadel
A & F Kaiser
Max Kalika
Neel Kar
George Karachalias
Karita
Martti Karonen, Inger Ekman
James Kasson
Alison Kates
Kate Katigbak
Michael B. Katz
Chris Kaufmann
Otavio Manzano Kavakama
Tom Kaye
Alexandra Keefe
Christine Keen
Kolbe Kegel
Keith
Joe Kendall
Adam Kennedy
Al Kennedy
Bill Kent
Clark Kent

Supporters

Pedro Kerplunk
Alhussein Khalil
Dan Kieran
Carl Kimlinger
Reverend Kevin King
Samuel Kinns
Gwen Kirby
Asher Klein
Harry Klein
Zak Klein
John Kleist
Jo Kling
Chris Klinowski
Mia Kloppmann
David Klueger
Anastasia Knasiak
Jesse Knee
Kristjan Knight
Jorden Kolding
John Krainski
Lukas Kristjanson
Aaron Krukow
Andy "The Tongue" Kubiak
Laryn Kuchta
Todd Kuhl
Mikko J. Kuosa
Philip Kuruvilla
ChernYue Kwok
Micki L-R, D'Nancy Johnson

Dave Laban
Dr. Crazy Cat Lady
JP LaFond
Tony Laidig
Alan Laing
Omah Laird
Luc Lajoie
Vivian Lam
Matthew Lambek
Dario Landazuri
Stacy Lane
Langoustaphiliac
Peter Langstaff
firstName lastName
Zachary Laughrey
Mathias Balle Lauridsen
Amy Lawson
Nicola Lawson
Greg Lazarev
LC from bklyn
Daniel Leaning
Christopher Lee
Ethan Lee
Kieran Lee
Pete Lee
Erik Leffingwell
Jacqueline Lemay
Eoin Lennon
Ron Levin
Warren Levinson

Joey Levy
Andy Lewis
Graham Lewis
Anthony Li
Mengwen Li
Tony Liang
Supriya Limaye
Dan Linden
Tom Littler
David Lloyd
Kim Lloyd
Peter Lloyd
LNZAva
Beth Lockhart
Alan Lodge
David Loetz
Eric Logan
Lois & Ethan
Emma Lok
Hannah Lomax-Vogt
Stoo Lombard-Cook
Philip Lorenson
Phoebe Lumley
Ben Lund-Conlon
Colin Lunt
Helen Lynch, Susie Lynch-Babb
Paul Lyon
Shawn Lyons
Dan M

Supporters

m -
Mike Machin
Euan MacInnes
James Mackenzie-Thorpe
Gregor MacLennan
Malcolm Macleod
Hannah Madden
Trygve Madsen
Arturo Magidin
Mark Magnee
Mwaki Magotswi
Anne Maguire
Al-Wakkass Mahmood
Thomas Mahoney
Andrew Main
Kelso Mallette
David Malone
Simon Malpass
Calogero Maniscalco
Nicholas Manktelow
Summer Manning
Kevin Maples
Marc Eugene Marcotte
Sarah Marcotte
Andrew L. Marcus, D. Zachary Brazdil
Shoshanah Marohn
Liz Marriner
Michael Marsh
Chris Marshall
Ian Marshall
Chris Martin
Francis Martin
Paul Martin
Scott Matheson
Katy Matthews
Madeline Matthews
Drew Mayo
Alicia McBride
Mark McCann
Grace McClintock
Grant McConnon
Chris McCormack
Lisa McCorvie
Kent McCrea
Steve McCrea
Marshall McCutchen
Michael McDonough
Dan McGing
Devan McGranahan
Hillary McGraw
Justin McGuire
Steve McIntosh
Gavin McKeown
Daniel Mckinnell
Stephen McLaughlin
Stephen McLaughlin
Cat McLoughlin
Isobel McMahon
Julia McMurray
Me
Derek Meade
Megan
William Meldrum
Alex Melnick
William R. Mendelsohn
Nino Mendolia
Freddie Mewcury
Stefan Michel
Tracy Middlebrook, Alison Rickey
Jonathan Miles
Simon Miles
Lance Milham
Jon Miller
Meredith Miller
Tom Miller
Renée Millette
Julia Mills
Minerva and Saffron (Cats)
Sarah Minsloff
Miriam and Dave

Supporters

Catriona Mitchell
Clive Mitchell
Mark Mitchell
Olivia "Sylv" Mitchell,
Alex "Mitch" Mitchell
John Mitchinson
Si MnMoffatt
Bryan Mock
Noah Mogey
Katie Monaco
Stephanie Monaco
Manda Moncada
Anders Montonen
Erin Moodie
Meghan Moore
Rog Moore
Simon Moore
John Moore-Weiss
Ghost Moose
Matt Moretti
Ed Morrish
Steven Morrison
Gwynne E Morrissey
Eric Moseley
Nathan Mosher
Andre Mostert
Sam Mould
Stephen Moylan
Barry Muise
Charlie Mulholland
Paul Mullen
David Mulvaney
David Mulvee
Andrew Mundell
Delia Muresan
Jason Murphy
Edel Murray
Margaret Murray
Sean Murray
Belinda Mustoe
Allan Myrick
James Nathan
Andrew Nattan
Carlo Navato
Thomas Neill
Eric Nelson
Kit Nelson
Sarah Nelson
Laura Nerenberg
Michael Nesser
Martin Neville
Rachael Nevins
Craig Newmark
Pete Newton
Ian Nicholls
Eva Nickelson
Mike Nimmo
Phil Niro
Ted Nitz
Thabo "Cheese" Nkuebe
Timothy Nockalls
Joonas Nõmmelt
John Norman
Dean Norrie
Martyn Norris
Sean Nulty
Alex Numann
Jonny Numbers
Ann Nunnally
Fred Nuttall
Katelyn Lee Nykorak
Caitríona O'Brien
Shane O'Connell
Rob O'Connor
Fionnuala O'Driscoll
Craig O'Hara
Elizabeth O'Leary
Douglas O'Neill
Ciara O'Sullivan
Scott Oberg
Carver Akiteru Oblander
George Ogata
Ergo Ojasoo
Max Olds
Carl Olsen
Tim Oltmanns
David Osborne
Oscariano
Willow Ostler
Mary Owen

Supporters

Patrick Owen
Patrick Micheal Oxlong-Mckenna
Tam P
P_T_S
Marc Pacheco
Uxia Padin
Nikki Paige
Andrew Pain
Chris Palagy
David Palmer
Carter Paret
Ross Parfitt
Adam Parke
John Parke
Rodney Parker
Edward Parry
Tim Parsons
Hannah Pascal
Jaynesh Patel
Raj Patel
Kay Paterson-Bassett
Paul from NYC
Steve Payne
Simon Peacock
Kristian Peacocke
Rosamund Pearce
Paul Pearlman
Selina Pearson
Ant Pease
Robin Peel
Kate Pelletier
William Penn
J. L. Pennington
Jose Luis Perez
Craig Perl
Jen Pesek
Sanne Peters
Edward Petersen
Kevin Peterson
Anwar Petty
Miranda Phair
Joshua Phares
Michael Phelan
Jonathan Levi Phillips
Stephen Pick
Amy Pickard
kEn Pike \:D
Štěpán Pilař
Marlène Magalhaes Pinto
Lynda Salem Poling
Berwyn Pollard
Justin Pollard
Pips Pollard
Mark Pope
John Potts
Kara Potts
Justin Power
Andrew Powers
Stephen Pratt
David Price
Ian Price
Lee Priestley
Tom Pritchard
Megan Procario
Joshua Proctor
Shaun Pryszlak
David Purvis
Bel Pye
Nicholas Pyeatt
Christian Queisser
Edward Radue
Brian Ramsay
Sarah Rand
Daniel Randall
Erin Ratz
Raheel Razvi
Rachel Read
Michael Ready
Bradford Reagon
John Reck
Tony Redican
Joshua Redmond
Laurel Redmond
Neil Redmond
John Reesman
Phillip Reeves
Terri Reeves
Michael (Micky) Reich
Sandra Reid
Stephen Reid
Timothy Reid
Bas Reijers
Derek Reise

Supporters

Bryony Retter
Kevin Revell
Steve Rewinski
Timothy Rezendes
Peter Rhodes
Tom Rhodes
Adam Rich
Jonny Richards
Jaye Richardson
Nick Richardson
Peter Richardson
Max Richie
Angela Ricker
David Rigby
Joseph Riley
Eduardo Rios
Rudy Riske
Cathy Rivard
John Rivett
Antoine "Griezy" Griezmann Rivoire-Gavranovic
Kelly Roark-Belcher
Wyn Roberts
Emily Robertson
Phoenix Robins
Matthew Kyle Rockett
Timothy Rogers
Carmen Romano
Anton Römer
Rooney
Mic Ros
Frank Leon Rose
Patrick Rose
Phillip Rose
Sam Rose
Philip Rothfeld
Kate Rothwell
Sophie Rottenbach
Esther and Tim Roughsedge
Janet Rowe
Matthew Rowell
Patrick Rowland
Coral Rubble & Sandy Overlay
Judith Rubin
Michael Ruhno
Corinne Rupp
Thomas Rushton
Benjamin L Russell
Mark Russell
Erik Ruud
George Ryall
Arne Rydell
Lexi Ryedale
Almaeron S
Beth S
Krish S
Vanessa R. Saavedra
Justin Saber
Chris Sable
Chris Sadowski, Rose Turner
Gursimran Sahota
Katariina Salonen
Michael Salter
Kaushik Sambamurthy
Victoria Guadalupe Sanchez
Charcole Sarar
Frances Sarrel
Rodney Sauer
Daniel Saunders
Jez Sawyer
Adam Schawel
Peter Schlemmer
Kurtis Schmidt
Sandra Schmidt
Rhys Schmidtke
Mike Schneider
Philip Schnell, Kara Gniewek
Gabriel Schofield
Sander Scholtus
Keith Schon
Joseph Schramm
Fides Schwartz
Hillel Schwartz
Liz Schwartz

Supporters

Zack Schwartz, Cassie Scarlett
Yaniv Schwerin
Bruce Scott
Katherine Scott
Lauren Seales
Adele Seelke
Dan Settle
Alex Sewell
Karan Shah
Laurel Shane
Jonathan Shapiro
Rajat Sharma
Margaret Shaw
David Sheffer
Darran Shepherd
David Shepherd
Wendell Shepherd
Shane Sheridan
Andrea Sholler and Bart Mosley
Sarah Shonbrun
Phil Shoobridge
Richard shore
Andy Shorten
Bartosz Siepracki
Robert Sillitoe
Kevin Silvester
Anthony C Simmons
Catherine Simpson
Steve Simpson
Joshua Sincoskie
Manpreet Singh
Clare Singline
Alex Siri
Samantha Slater
Alan Sloan
Maria Slocombe
Nic Small
Amy Smith
Andrew Smith
George Smith
Jonathan Smith
Luke Smith
Sarah D. Smith
Stew Smith
Adam Smout
Lucas Snider
Lake So
Jason Sobolewski
Dev Sodagar
Don Sorcinelli
Ian Sorensen
Stephen P Spackman
Jeff Spakowksi
Geoffrey Spear
Michelle Spencer
Stephen Spinks
Michelle Spitzer
Andrea Stancin
James Stanford
Kevin Stanton
David Stapel
Rachel Stechman
Gavin Steed
Andrew Steele
Gordon Stephen
Rob Stephens
Benjamin Stevens
Laurel Stevens
Jonathan Stewart
Andy Stockdale
Matt Stone
Joseph Storm
Henning Strack
Janet Strath
Renata Strause
Andrew Straw
Leonie Strawbridge
Samantha Streeter
Struan Stringer-Wright
Ebbe Stubbe
John F. Suggs
Becky Sunflower
Alexa Sussmane
Pete Sutton
Mari Svolsbru
Terry Swann
Emily Sweet
Michael Swift
Peter Swinburne
Karen Sylvester
Lesley Szostek
Nick T

Supporters

Steve T
Richard Tammar
Garrett Tanner
Several Tardigrades
Charles Taylor
Kenneth Taylor
Shaun Taylor
Thomas Taylor
Thomas Tebalt
Schwarzer Teufelshund
Bruce Thai
The Farttman Family
The Law Office of Steve Seal LLC
thedickgrant
thehardmenpath
Empress Theodora
Oliver Thiessen
Morgan Thistle
Aaron Thomas
Leivur Thomassen
David Thompson
Lilli Thompson
Michael Thompson
Robert Thompson
Robert Thompson
Scott Thompson
Will Thompson
Julia Thomson
Verity Thomson
Vic Thor
Lyndall Thorn
Joseph R Thorne
Kevin Thornton
Katrina Tipton
Dr Mantis Toboggan
Erin Todd
Andrew Tolliday
Hank Torino
Jakob Storm Tråsdahl
Alan Trewartha
Matthew Trigg
Charlie Tuff
David Tully
James Tunnicliffe
L.F. Turner
Neil Turner
Sarah Tuttleton
Brian Uiga
Amir Unger
Devona Upurok
Jonathan & Larissa Ursprung
Frank Usbeck
Mait Uus
Thanik Vadivelu
Richard Valentine
Daniel Vallender
Elysia Van Deusen
Michon van Dooren
Jeffrey van Kruijssen
Quinn Van Order
Jane Van Susteren
Celysse van Zyl
Kevin VanMetre
Dave Vass
Alexander Veljanovski
Karla Velmin
Bob Venanzi
Tom Vesters
Faye and Jon Vile
Vera Vilhjalmsdottir
Vincent, the Virginal Viking Viscount
Vintage Youth Cricket Club
Jose Vizcaino
Aaron Vizzini
The Countess von Voight, The Duchess of Twiss
James Vortkamp-Tong
Steve Vrbancic
Charly W
R W

Supporters

Steve Wagner
Morgan Wahl
D'John Wainwright
George Walden
Mark Wales
Emma Walker
Felicia Walker
Max Walter
Zak Walter
Brian Walters & Viktorija Gjorgievska
Aaron Wang
Andrew Ward
Matthew Ward
Simon Ward
Alex Wareham
Guy Warner
Renen Wasserman
Vicky Wastell
Keith Waters
William Waterstreet
Adriel Watt
Christina Watts
Jeffrey M. Watts
David Webb
Dillon Webster
Steven Webster
Steven Weckert
Brian Weigus
Benjamin Weiss
William Welborn
Chase Welch
Robert Wells
Bat Wench (Mau Craze-Gray)
Daniel Wesely
Anthony West
Hannah West
Beatrice Weston
Bea Weston, Barny Weston
Doug Wheaton
Paul Whelan
Hillary White
Joseph White
Nigel White
Stu White
Sean Whitear
Lish Whitson
Kate H Whittle
Darren Whitworth
Catherine Wick
Sarah Wickham
Jesse Wiener
P.T. Wilding
Nathan Wilgeroth
Peter Wilkin
Tim Wilkinson
KW Willett
Danielle Williams
Gareth Williams
Julia Williams
Phil Williams
David Wilmot
Dominic Wilson
Lydia Wilson
Sofie Wilson
Stuart Wilson
Thomas and MaryAnn Wiltshire
Natalie Winters
Helen Wischnewski
Julia Wither
John-Wayne Witt
Michael Wojcik
Georgia Wolfe
Carl Wolter
Andrew Womack
Marcus Wong
Joshua Wood
Miel Wood
Noah Wood
Sarah Woodford
Jake Woods
Nick Wookey
Benjamin Wooller
Peter Worthington
Tim Worwood
John Wright
Kristofer Wright
MJ Wright
Wrikken
David Wynne

Supporters

Isla Yager
David Yarrow
Chern Yue
Tom Yue
Maria Zahorcova

Brianna Zarlinga
Jane Zavisca
Thierry Zell
Kevin Zinsmeister

Patrick Zlatopolsky
Zoey
Qian Zy

A Note on the Author

Alice Fraser shuttles her family between London, small-town Queensland and alternate dimensions in an attempt to get the best and worst of all worlds. She grew up halfway between suburban Sydney and her own imagination, raised as a Burmese Buddhist by an ex-Catholic and a Jew. She has been named one of the *Telegraph*'s top fifty comedians of the twenty-first century and her stand-up comedy specials are on Amazon Prime, NextUp and the ABC. She has a number of bestselling audio documentaries on Audible and has produced two critically acclaimed babies.

A Note on the Type

The text of this book is set in Centaur MT Pro. Based on the Renaissance-period printing of Nicolas Jenson from around 1470, it was designed by Bruce Rogers and paired with an italic designed by the calligrapher Frederic Warde, whose work was inspired by the calligraphy of Ludovico Vicentino degli Arrighi. Released in 1929, Centaur shows some of the irregularities of early type compared to later designs, including the slanted horizontal stroke of the 'e' and the off-centre dots above the 'i' and the 'j'.